Castle of
Closing Doors

Also by Daoma Winston
in Thorndike Large Print ®

The Mayeroni Myth
The Carnaby Curse

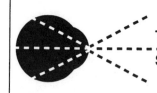

This Large Print Book carries the
Seal of Approval of N.A.V.H.

Castle of Closing Doors

Daoma Winston

Thorndike Press • Thorndike, Maine

Library of Congress Cataloging in Publication Data:

Winston, Daoma, 1922-
   Castle of closing doors / Daoma Winston.
      p.   cm.
   ISBN 1-56054-516-X (alk. paper : lg. print)
   1. Large type books.   I. Title.
[PS3545.I7612C375   1993]   92-36457
813'.54—dc20   CIP

Thorndike Large Print® Romance Series edition published
in 1993 by arrangement with Jay Garon Brooke
Associates, Inc.

Cover photo by Tom Knobloch.

The tree indicium is a trademark of Thorndike Press.

This book is printed on acid-free, high opacity paper. ∞

For
Ann Nelson Mosettig
who came in at the beginning

Chapter One

Stacey did not know why she gave up hope, surrendered her dream of love at that particular moment.

It was, in content and quality, no different from all the others that had come and gone since her arrival at the Casa de Sombra three weeks before, when riding through the tall cedar gates with Derek, her joy had turned to awe and she whispered, "Is this really home?" And he answering merely, "Yes." He said, "Yes" — just that — in a stranger's voice, all his sweet, cherishing laughter wiped away.

The orchids he had bought her in Juarez seemed suddenly wilted. The warm afternoon air was edged with chill. Stacey, instantly responsive, felt then for the first time that sense of isolation from him, from everyone around her, which was to become a condition of her days.

She was alone, bewildered, but she accepted what came as it came; still hopeful that soon the Derek she had married only a little more than two months before — that charming, impetuous, loving Derek — would return to replace the sarcastic, indifferent stranger he had become as they drove through the tall cedar gates.

There had been worse moments, so many of them, and each burned into her memory like acid on living flesh, that she no longer tried to find meaning in them.

She clung blindly through all of them to one thought. Derek had loved her, married her, and brought her home with him.

But then, quite suddenly, she gave up hope, surrendered her dream of love. She didn't know why it happened at that moment. She knew only that for the first time she was *afraid*.

They were in the huge dining room.

The chandelier made prismed reflections on the polished table top, where woven place mats were islands of subdued color. Flickering candles cast gleaming highlights on the old silver, the fine china, the crystal goblets.

The others at the table with her, the four arrayed against her, she suddenly realized, took for granted the luxury of the cedar-scented room. They were accustomed to the thick carpets, the huge carved furniture. They had lived in luxury always. But to Stacey, who had never experienced it before, it was a burden she was not prepared to carry — a symbol of her position. She was a sparrow among swans. She did not belong in that family, in that house. Perhaps that was what had been wrong from the beginning. It no longer seemed to matter.

She saw Elena, who sat at her right, and Derek, who sat at her left, raise dark, smiling eyes and look at each other in the mysterious complicity of twinhood.

Some soft, primitive voice whispered wordlessly inside Stacey, murmured a vague warning against an unnamed threat. She sat very still, waiting. But nothing happened. Elena and Derek, brother and sister twin, simply smiled at each other. That was all.

Elena was beautiful. Her black hair was rolled into a shining coronet. Her dark eyes slanted over high cheekbones. Under the dull light of the chandelier, the soft glow of the candles, her skin was like pearl against her red velvet gown.

Stacey, at first disconcerted to find that Derek and Elena were so much alike, had taken some comfort in the small differences between them that she eventually noticed. They were both tall and slim, with the same coloring. They both had faces peculiarly untouched by time, although they were twenty-seven. But Elena's mouth, though it smiled easily, was more firm, her jaw slightly more squared than Derek's. So they were not quite the same.

But when they looked at each other in that

smiling conspiracy of which Stacey suddenly knew she was to be the victim, there was no comfort for her in the small differences between them. They were as one, allied in looks and in intent.

Stacey could no longer pretend to herself that only the politely-controlled opposition of the others to Derek's unexpected marriage had soured the sweetness of the welcome she had hoped for. Derek himself regretted their whirlwind courtship, the breathless joy which had seemed a promise of the future. Yet, if he had loved her ever, could that love so soon have died? And if he had not loved her, then why? Why the sweet kisses, the pursuits, and persuasion? Why had he brought her home with him? She didn't know. But the soft, primitive voice inside her whispered, — in words now — that whatever Derek did was done with reason.

That recognition sent a shiver through her. She made a small, involuntary movement. A heavy silver spoon spun away from her cold fingers, making a terrible clatter in the silence. The spoon finally came to rest, and stillness claimed the room again.

The attention that Stacey preferred to avoid was drawn to her. The Alexanders all turned and looked at her.

There was nothing to be done except wish

that she were invisible, and to apologize. "I'm sorry," she murmured, hoping that her sudden fear — full-blown in that moment — didn't color her voice.

"Is something wrong?" Elena asked. "Shall I ring for Henry?"

Stacey shook her head. Her sandy hair was cut very short, and woven through with golden strands, as if streaked with living sunlight. She had blue eyes, wide, candid, fringed with sooty black lashes, and arched black brows. The blackness of lash and brow, contrasting with her hair, gave her face a piquant quality which she herself had never noticed. Her skin was very light, a few freckles on her small straight nose, on her cheeks. Her mouth was sharply defined, naturally pink. She was exceptionally pretty without knowing it, without caring about it, which was odd in a twenty-two year old girl.

Derek, as always, following Elena's lead, demanded coldly, "Well? Is there something wrong?"

"No, of course not," Stacey told him.

The false warmth of a false smile brightened Elena's face. "Don't mind him, Stacey. It's just his nerves." She looked at Derek and he looked at her.

From across the table, the two other Alexanders continued to stare at Stacey.

11

She wondered if her earlier thoughts had turned her freckles green, but the levity was no more than habit. She had to tense herself to keep from shrinking under the steady regard of Richard's grim gray eyes. He was the middle brother, thirty, and so completely different from the twins that they might not have been related at all. His gray eyes, the color of fresh-laid cement, dominated his face. His dark hair was unruly. There were grooves in his tanned forehead, faint wrinkles at the corners of his eyes. There were marks on his cheeks that might become dimples. She wasn't sure though, for she had rarely seen him smile. But she had seen a watchful waiting look, seen it always.

It was there when he gravely handed her the offending silver spoon, saying, "You might need this."

She accepted it, thanked him. Her cold fingers carefully placed the spoon in line with the others beside her plate.

Richard didn't reply to her thanks.

But the fourth and oldest Alexander, whose name was John, lolling in the chair beside Richard, doing all his smiling for him, laughed hoarsely, "Stacey, my dear, you are pretty enough to be allowed a small social error. But not pretty enough to look as if you've seen a ghost at the table with you."

Then she knew that the strange quiver of fright she had felt inside her had been reflected on her face and he had observed it. Quickly, she forced a smile. She thanked him for his compliment. But she knew, from other nights, that having finished the food he so hugely enjoyed, and having paid her a ritual gallantry, he was ready to begin that polite inquisition to which she had been subjected ever since she arrived at the Casa de Sombra . . .

House of Shadow . . .

It was well named, she thought. Even within the dining room, under the light of the chandelier, she felt the burden of the shadow upon her.

"You say you were born in Baltimore?" John asked, taking a last sip of wine from his crystal goblet.

"Yes. In Baltimore, John."

"And you've lived there all your life?"

"Yes, I did."

"There are a lot of sailors in Baltimore, aren't there?"

Confused, wondering why he should ask that, she said, "I don't know."

"You don't?" He fingered his red silk ascot, smoothed his black vest over his paunch. "If you'd really lived there, you ought to know, oughtn't you?"

She couldn't help herself. Knowing that it

was useless, she turned, nevertheless, to Derek in mute appeal. But Derek, as indifferent as always, ignored her.

John, pursing his red lips under his thick black mustache, went on, "It's odd that you should deny knowing sailors, Stacey, my dear."

She didn't answer him. It hardly seemed necessary. They had been over the same ground many times, though she didn't remember that he'd ever mentioned sailors before.

His questions had always bewildered her, but now she looked into the black slits of his eyes and her fear quickened.

She sat, quite alone, on one side of the long table. The Alexanders, as one unit, faced her. She was being accused of some undescribed crime. John, forty, stout, red-faced, and always smiling, spoke for them all as grand inquisitor.

"Sailors come and go," he said. "They have girls in every port."

"I never knew any, not at all," she said finally.

"Ah, you didn't? And from Baltimore, you went to Mexico?"

"I told you. The tour. It seemed an exciting thing to do."

"You do like excitement, Stacey?"

"Sometimes." She confessed it as if it were a fault.

But he continued to smile. "And how many times did you go to Mexico?"

"I've told you that. Three times." Her voice sharpened. "And yes, I went with Marcia Bellows."

John nodded approval. "Very quick of you to know what I was going to ask next."

Though his voice was kindly, though he beamed at her, she knew, as she had known from the first moment that she met him, that John Alexander had been shocked to meet her and had loathed her on sight. And what held for John held even more strongly for Elena. Their mock friendliness, interest, was a thin veneer over well-concealed rage, which had surprised her, hurt her, but never deceived her.

But Richard — Richard who rarely spoke, rarely smiled, who leaned toward her now with that watchful waiting look — was the enigma. She couldn't read him. She wasn't sure that she wanted to.

Henry, the Indian servant, carried in a silver coffee service and set it before Elena.

He was a short man, broad, solid. His coarse black hair was braided and just touched his shoulders. His face was ageless, expressionless, swarthy. He wore a long-sleeved cotton

15

shirt, blue jeans, and deerskin moccasins. He turned a slow black glance on John, on Richard, then silently left the room.

Stacey's moment of respite was over.

John asked, "So you've been in Mexico three times in the past year?"

"Yes. Assistant tour director. With Marcia Bellows. I told you. Three times. I think that's right."

"You *think* that's right? Aren't you sure?"

"I am," she said, desperation putting an edge in her voice. "I just meant . . . oh, never mind. I *am* sure, John."

"How did you meet Miss Bellows?" Richard asked.

Stacey looked at him, surprised. It was the first time he had joined John in questioning her.

Elena asked gently, "You do remember that, don't you, Stacey?"

"Well?" Derek demanded, "why don't you tell them?"

Stacey suddenly remembered a kitten she had once seen, pitied, and rescued. A bronze kitten with a pointed face, small, fluffy, and sweet, harassed by a circle of dogs. Harried, backed against a garage wall, while the dogs barked, edged in, nerving themselves for a final attack. She was that kitten now.

She cried in sudden defiance, "But I've already told them a dozen times, Derek."

"Why not once more?" John asked. "Don't you like to talk about your past? Do you have something to hide?"

She didn't have to answer.

Elena, lovely in the candlelight, leaned toward her, said earnestly, "Why, I thought you understood. We *are* Derek's family. We have the right, the duty, to consider your background." She paused to pass filled coffee cups to Stacey first, then to the men, in a perfect parody of good manners. With that gracefully done, she smiled at Stacey. "You don't understand truly, of course. We are the Alexanders. One of the oldest families in the state. We are something, stand for something."

"Is that why you . . ." The words, once begun, could not be withdrawn. Stacey forced herself to go on. "Is that why you keep asking me the same questions?"

"Of course," John said silkily. "Why else?"

Her wide blue eyes met his narrowed stare.

She had believed that at first, believed it until that very evening. But she believed it no longer.

The questions were to trap her, to prove her a liar. But why?

"Except for familial interest, why should we care?" John asked.

She looked down at her coffee, whispered,

"I don't know."

"Silly child," John told her, suddenly indulgent. "Try to forgive us our odd ways, if you can. The Alexanders . . ."

Richard broke in, his voice harsh, "You've been over that a few thousand times, too, John."

The Comanche, called that as if she had no other name, served caramel custard in cut-glass dishes, ignoring the conversation. Her hair was black, touched with strands of gray, and cut in straight bangs across her wide forehead and straight around her head at ear length. Her eyes were small, obsidian-black, and slanted in pads of fat. Her mouth was almost lipless, and often open, exposing the gap made by four missing front teeth. She was Henry's wife, and with their eighteen-year-old daughter Maria, ran the big house with surprising efficiency. Stacey often wondered how the three of them managed it.

The Comanche retreated as quietly as she had come.

Derek said, "Stacey, if you are quite through, you can go to your room now."

It had happened before, of course. The sudden dismissal, the same words, in the same indifferent voice. Yet it still had the power to wound her. Even then — with hope gone, replaced by fear — it could hurt her.

18

Stacey rose at once, her cheeks burning.

John laughed, "My dear, if you will be lonely, just confess it to me. I'll gladly come and join you. Between us we'll make the hours pass."

She knew that the teasing was pretense only. She had learned to dodge the brotherly little pats that were too much like stolen caresses. She recognized the twinkle in his eyes as a lecherous glint which he never bothered to conceal, even from Derek, who plainly didn't object. Laughingly, Derek had told her that John had a well-developed taste for good food, good wine, and bad women. Since she didn't qualify as any of the three, Stacey wished that John would leave her alone.

But now he heaved his bulk up, a gesture full of courtliness but no grace.

"Act your age, John," Richard told him, but with grim gray eyes on Stacey.

She murmured, "Good night. Excuse me." And fled like a well-trained child.

She hurried across the big rectangular patio.

Night wind rustled in the tall hollyhocks, and long shadows swayed in the faint oblongs of light that marked the draped windows.

The whisper of her footsteps seemed to have an echo, as if someone were following her. She looked, but no one was there.

She was gasping, breathless, by the time she

reached her room, hers alone — the cell to which Derek had consigned her. She flung the door open, relieved to have gained sanctuary. But as golden light flowed out to enfold her in spurious welcome, she froze at the threshold.

Chapter Two

Maria, the young Indian girl, stood before the mirror. She seemed so entranced by her reflection that she didn't hear the sound of the opening door, nor Stacey's gasp of surprise.

Maria was small, very shapely. She wore a white off-the-shoulder blouse tucked into a wide pleated squaw skirt of rainbow colors. A black belt cinched tightly showed off her narrow waist, her swelling breasts. Her hair was long, a coarse dull black, and dropped in a great fall to her round hips from a tiny knot of red ribbon. On her head, perched smartly over her right eye, she wore a small, white overseas cap, on which was embroidered the words "Tour Director."

Stacey's cap — the one she had been wearing when she first met Derek.

Maria preened, smiled at herself, and the face which Stacey had thought to be stolid, expressionless, glowed with self-satisfaction.

Stacey drew a long, slow breath. "Maria," she said softly, "I've asked you before to let my things alone."

Maria gave herself a last fond look in the mirror. She turned slowly, and just as slowly the self-satisfaction was wiped away. When she faced Stacey, her round cheeks had settled into their usual impassive mold and her black eyes were empty. "It is a nice hat. I would not hurt it."

"I know." Stacey felt ashamed, somehow in the wrong. She went on helplessly, "But last time it was my dress, now this . . . and I asked you . . ."

"I have not hurt *them*." She took off the hat, dropped it on the dresser top, and went past Stacey in a swift, gliding walk. "Nor you. I am the one."

She glided into the shadows and became one with them.

Stacey, on the threshold, within the glow of the yellow light, was alone with Maria's words echoing in her mind.

She went in, closed the door.

The silence of the big room seemed to mock her. Maria's words rebounded from the dark, heavy, carved pieces of Spanish Colonial furniture in which at first Stacey had taken a great deal of pleasure.

I have not hurt them. Nor you. I am the one, Maria had said, her black eyes suddenly aglow, as if red embers behind them had been touched by the breeze of hate.

Maria hated Stacey, feared her, and defied her. Yet the words implied that she, not Stacey, had been hurt.

How? Stacey asked herself. What had she done to Maria? What did it mean?

Before that evening, before she had seen the smiling glance of complicity exchanged between Derek and Elena, Stacey had asked herself questions. But those had been other questions.

She wondered what she had done to alienate Derek hardly more than two months after their marriage. She wondered why all the Alexanders found her to be so unsatisfactory an addition to their family. Why even the three Indian servants were against her.

It was easy for her to assume that the fault was hers. Orphaned as an infant, raised in a dozen different foster homes, she had been trained early to accept her own inadequacies, her own flaws, as the explanation for whatever came her way.

But now, suddenly, she looked beyond herself for the answers to new questions.

Why had Derek changed the moment they drove through the cedar gates of the Casa de Sombra?

Why had he sent her to stay alone, alone in the room that had become her cell and then her sanctuary?

Why did John, Richard, Elena demand ridiculous details about her background, subject her to a continuous catechism of all that she wanted most to forget?

Bewilderment rounding her wide blue eyes, she looked at the room, as if it — if it would — could tell her.

She noticed the small white cap. A smile touched her lips. It had been her passport out of drabness and into adventure. With that thought, her smile faded. That same small white cap had been her passport from adventure into a danger she couldn't name.

She turned away. She lit the prepared kindling in the fireplace, knowing that the quick, dancing flames would not warm her. The chill she felt was from within. Neither the fire's heat, nor the snug weight of the quilt which she wrapped around her narrow shoulders, could touch it.

She curled up on the huge, canopied bed, its blue velvet roof the screen on which she projected her memories . . .

By the third tour, her earlier excitement had worn off. But she was still grateful to Marcia Bellows for having given her the opportunity to escape the humdrum file clerk job which had supported her until then.

Marcia was about forty-five, a plump, fast-talking former actress, with obviously-dyed red hair, and warm brown eyes. She knew Spanish, knew Mexico from one end to the other, and on tour, performed constantly, spouting jokes, history, and news.

Stacey, as her assistant, was responsible for counting the noses of elderly school teachers as they entered the bus in Merida, and counting the same noses when they returned from visiting the ruins at Chichen Itza. She was responsible for providing bicarbonate of soda, and milk of magnesia, and suntan lotion in Acapulco, and for retrieving lost flight bags, umbrellas, and glasses in Mexico City.

She met Derek at Teotihuacan, on the steps of the Aztec pyramids. She was trying to entertain the usual few elderly ladies who were too tired to climb up to the platform at the top. She noticed a tall, very handsome young man walking about restlessly, who seemed more interested in the people there than in the pyramids themselves. So that when he paused to ask her to take a picture of him, she was hardly surprised. And when he remained to chat with her, she decided that he must be homesick. He delighted the elderly ladies, and finally, with perfect aplomb, virtually joined the tour. He did it on his own terms, simply following the bus, first from Mexico City to Cuernavaca, from there to Taxco, and then to Toluca, before following it back to Mexico City. He drove his own car, appeared to tease the elderly ladies; then disappeared until they were bedded down, and

Stacey was free to drink tequila by silver moonlight, to dance the rumba under the stars, to walk in the sweet, orchid-scented air.

He was tall, lithe. His dark hair was brushed into a smooth, shining cap. His dark eyes shone with laughter, his smile was warm, endearing.

To Stacey, who had never known love before, he was that miracle of which every girl dreams. The courtship, a ten-day whirlwind of laughter and kisses, ended with his proposal and Stacey's acceptance. Marcia, until then pleased, was suddenly disapproving, offered perturbed warnings, which Stacey, aglow with joy, immediately forgot.

The day that Marcia, tour in tow, flew back to Baltimore, Derek and Stacey were married. Aside from the few offhand comments he had made about his family, wealth, and home, she knew next to nothing about him.

That didn't matter. They set out on a two-month honeymoon, traveling by car, which took them the length and breadth of Mexico. She was too bemused by love, then, to wonder why they drove so aimlessly, often recrossing their path; why he chose grimy inns for their overnight stops; even why he so often left her waiting anxiously for his return while he went out to walk alone. At the end of those two months they drove north, crossed into the

United States at Juarez. She was wearing the great mass of orchids he had bought her. He bent to kiss her as they were waved on by the El Paso customs officials.

They continued driving north through bright blinding sunlight until in the mountains of northern New Mexico, where sage and cedar spread patterns of grays and greens on the raw red earth, they passed through a tiny village called Piedras; and went beyond it, following a ribbon dirt road that climbed and circled and curved to lead to a small ravine.

There, placed squarely within that cleft was a huge walled adobe house. Above it, the sky was blue, the mountain ridges streaked with brilliant sun. But the house itself was shrouded in heavy shadow, shadow which she later realized was perpetual except for brief moments each day at noon — Shadow which had given the house its name — the Casa de Sombra.

Derek stopped before tall cedar gates, blew his horn low and long, and then the gates slowly swung inward.

As they drove through, Stacey, having never had a place where she belonged before, full of joy that quickly became awe, asked, "Derek, is this home?"

"Yes," he said in the blank, cold voice of a stranger.

Suddenly she felt alone, peculiarly alienated

from him. She touched his hand, hoping for reassurance. He drew away from her. That was the beginning.

Behind them, the tall gates swung shut on great iron hinges.

The house was formed by three wings, a long center one and two shorter ones, making a wide-based U. Its tan adobe was smooth and uncracked. Heavy cedar vegas extending from the flat roof were oiled a dark brown. The roof was built beyond the face of the building, and all the way around it, covered a path neatly lined with hollyhocks. The portale — that part of the roof which covered the path — the brown vegas, even the hollyhocks, made the house seem familiar. It was like some that Stacey had seen in Mexico, except that it was larger.

The patio, too, was large, a wide and long rectangle of unplanted dusty red earth. At its center, there was an old well, surrounded by more straggly hollyhocks of red, pink, and white. A huge, rusty bucket sat on the well's edge, a thick rope running from it around the wheel pulley at its top. A curved iron bench was nearby.

"It's beautiful," Stacey said finally, turning from her study of the house to Derek.

Without answering, he got out of the car. After a moment, she followed him.

Henry was waiting, his wrinkled face stolid.

She had seen many Indians in Mexico, but never before in the United States. She wondered if he spoke English, and delighted in his appearance.

In a moment, The Comanche waddled down to stand beside Henry.

Near them, stacked against the high wall, was a good-sized pile of adobe bricks, some the usual tan, a few pink. Close by was an old-fashioned Indian kiln.

The scene made a picture postcard, and she smiled joyfully as Derek introduced her, but the faces of the Indians remained stony. They acknowledged her with brief nods.

Then, as Derek led her under the portales, past the row of doors that lined the wing, one of them opened. Maria dashed out, her plump face dimpled. She stopped suddenly, her wide skirt swirling around her. "You are back," she said.

"Yes. And I've brought my wife with me," Derek answered.

He went on. With a smile at Maria, Stacey followed him, wondering at the quick fading of Maria's welcoming look.

The Indians came of a different culture, Stacey thought, and perhaps that was why all three of them seemed so strange, so impassive. But Maria was young, and spoke English.

Stacey decided that if she tried she could make friends with her, perhaps with the others, too.

Derek stopped before a heavy carved door. "This is the main part of the house. The living room, dining room, all of that. These rooms are connected to each other. Those in the two wings open only into the patio."

She smiled at him, relieved that he had finally spoken to her. "You sound like a tour director now."

With a brief glance at her, he opened the door and went ahead of her into the living room.

She had no time then, in the confusion of welcome, to notice its furnishings.

Elena and John were there, deep in a conversation that broke off when Derek grinned, "I'm back."

Elena jumped to her feet. She wore black riding trousers, shiny black boots, a white silk shirt tied at the throat with a red scarf.

She was beautiful, and so like Derek that Stacey was taken aback.

Elena, her voice soft, musical, cried, "Derek, why didn't you let us know you were on the way?"

He said, glancing at Stacey, "It didn't seem wise." He went on quickly to make the introductions.

There was a silence, a silence so brief that

Stacey wondered if she had imagined it.

Then Elena smiled, held out her hands. "What a lovely surprise! Welcome to Casa de Sombra."

John pushed himself out of a deep leather chair, advanced on Stacey, "The older brother has the privilege of kissing the bride." He kissed her, his mustache unpleasant to her lips, while his hand gave her a pat.

She backed away from him, thinking that his embrace was oddly unbrotherly.

"Where did you meet?" Elena was asking. "When? You must tell us all about it."

"I want to talk to you," Derek said. He took up a small brass bell, rang it. "Excuse us, Stacey."

In moments, Maria appeared.

Derek said, "Take Stacey to her room," and glanced at Elena. "The blue?"

"The blue. Yes, that would be best," Elena agreed.

"Will you go with Maria, please?" Derek said.

Stacey nodded. She followed Maria outside, across the patio.

The room to which Maria led her was big, beautifully decorated. It had carved furniture, blue draperies, a four-poster bed, canopied in blue. A wool rug woven with Indian designs covered the floor.

Maria didn't answer Stacey's comment about the design, and a few moments later, when Henry brought the luggage in from the car, she turned silently to do the unpacking.

Stacey, seeing her begin to fill all the drawers of the dresser, said, "Maybe you'd better leave some room for Derek's things."

Maria's hands went still, her fingers clutching the slips she held. "He is across the patio. In his own room."

Stacey's cheeks burned. She didn't answer Maria.

But the young Indian girl went on, "You will not be happy here. This is a bad house. You must go away."

It was, Stacey told herself, the faint foreign sound in Maria's speech that made the words a threat.

She smiled at Maria. "But I'm married to Derek. This is my home now. I belong here."

"I belong here," Maria retorted. "Not you!"

Stacey, startled, told herself that it was natural, that she a stranger, should be resented. She said only, "I hope that some day we'll be friends."

Maria turned back to the unpacking, finished it, and left.

Alone, Stacey wondered why she had been

given a room away from Derek. She decided it was no more than a mistake. Or perhaps later, he would have her things moved in.

Chapter Three

She waited for what seemed a long time for him to come to her, and when he didn't appear, she changed from her travel-wrinkled dress to a blue blouse and a narrow black skirt. She brushed her sun-sprinkled sandy curls and touched pink lipstick to her mouth, and went in search of him.

As soon as she entered it, she saw that the living room was empty. Nervously twisting her wedding ring, the small circle of gold that Derek had put on her finger, she went through an arched doorway, and found herself in what she knew must be the dining room. Derek wasn't there either, but as she turned to leave, a tall breakfront caught her eye. She crossed to look at the array of old weapons it held. Knives, hilts carved in strange designs. Guns, pearl-handled, wood-handled. She studied them, thinking that Marcia would love to know about them, and at the same time, uneasily twisting her wedding ring, until somehow it slipped off, bounced on the rug, and spun away under the breakfront.

There was nothing to do but lie down on the floor, to grope for it. And she did. And as she slid her searching fingers along the narrow space, she heard the door in the next room open. She heard Elena's low, musical voice and Derek's answering tones come closer.

"That much is safely done, at least," Elena was saying. "And now suppose you explain."

"I told you how it was. I had to do something, didn't I?"

"But taking such a chance."

Derek laughed. "No chance."

"You can't be sure," Elena answered thoughtfully. "We'll have to see."

"I'm telling you there's nothing to worry about."

"But this time, dear brother, your absolute self-confidence doesn't reassure me."

Their voices had grown louder.

By the time Stacey had at last clutched her ring, scrambled to her feet, Elena and Derek were in the doorway.

"What on earth?" Elena cried, dark eyes narrowed suspiciously.

Derek frowned. "What are you doing here?"

She held out the ring, then slipped it on her finger. "I was looking for you, and dropped my ring, and . . ."

"And what did you want?" he asked.

She glanced at Elena, hesitated.

"Well?" Derek insisted.

Finally, Stacey said, in what was almost a

whisper, "I wondered if . . . perhaps Maria made a mistake . . . or will you move to be with me? Or . . ."

"It was no mistake. We'll have separate rooms. I prefer it that way."

Stacey felt as if she had been slapped. She ducked her head, her cheeks burning again. But Elena stood there, listening. Stacey couldn't discuss it.

Derek turned, walked out.

But when Stacey started to follow him, Elena touched her arm. "Wait, let's have some tea together, shall we?"

It would have been rude to refuse, so Stacey agreed, and the two of them settled on a huge velvet sofa in the living room.

Elena rang the brass bell, and when The Comanche waddled in, told her what she wanted.

The Comanche gave Stacey a blank look, nodded at Elena, and waddled out. Within moments, Maria brought in a brass teapot on a brass tray. She served the tea in fine china cups, and acknowledging Elena's thanks, glided out of the room.

"There," Elena said, smiling. "Now we can talk." She paused. Then, "Tell me, Stacey, where were you born?"

It was thus that she began the first of the long inquisitions. She ended it, when Stacey, having answered honestly and in detail, blurted out, "But I don't understand. Why does all this matter, Elena?"

Elena's dark eyes seemed to seek an answer in her teacup. At last, she said, "It doesn't, of course. Not to you. But you see, Stacey, we are an old family, one of great wealth, of real importance in the state. And Derek . . ." Elena smiled suddenly, "You have learned, haven't you? How impulsive he is?"

"I see," Stacey said. And she thought that she *did* see.

She was a nobody, from nowhere. She wasn't good enough for Derek Alexander. Which explained why, though Elena and John had welcomed her with smiles and courtesies, she sensed suspicion, lack of warmth, reserve in them. She thought suddenly that the Indian servants looked down on her, too.

That night, after a slow, silent dinner (Stacey blaming herself for bringing the pall that had settled in the room), John, chuckling richly, also asked her questions; and when he had finally finished, Derek told her, in almost those words, to go to her room.

She was bewildered by the abrupt change in him. It was as if a stranger had come to inhabit his body. She wished herself in Mexico again, with Derek — the old Derek — and wept until she fell asleep. Toward dawn, she wakened to hear an infant's cry.

She asked about it when The Comanche served breakfast to the four of them.

Elena said, smiling, "You heard a baby? Impossible. We have no babies here."

"That's some imagination you have," Derek snorted.

And John, with an insinuating glint, asked, "Is that a wishful fancy?"

She didn't insist. She already knew that she couldn't convince them. But she decided that she had to talk to Derek, talk to him alone, at the first opportunity. The opportunity didn't come. As soon as the meal was over, Derek drove away with John.

Elena had a second cup of coffee with Stacey, explained, "Our investments, you know. Derek and John are kept quite busy. You must forgive him."

Late in the afternoon, watching from her window, Stacey saw him return, enter a room in the opposite patio. She hurried over, knocked, and at his answer went in.

It was another big room, filled with furniture similar to her own, but decorated in green velvet.

Derek was sitting at a desk. He looked at her for a moment. "Well, Stacey?"

She clasped her small hands in front of her, lowered her head. She didn't know how to begin. But at last, oddly breathless, she asked, "Derek, what have I done?"

"Nothing at all. Why?"

She saw faint amusement in his dark eyes, and was suddenly angry. "Why?" she repeated. "That's ridiculous. I should be asking that. Why must I be in a separate room from you? Why did you humiliate me by sending me out of the dining room last night? Why . . ."

"Stacey, please." Derek frowned. "You've been here hardly a full twenty-four hours, and you're already complaining."

"But, Derek . . ."

"You have a lovely home. Soon I'll see to it that you have beautiful clothes."

"I didn't come here for a home or for clothes. I came to be with you," she cried.

"It happens that I'm busy after being away so long, Stacey." He paused. "And I suppose I should have told you before, but I prefer that you keep to your own wing. There is no reason for you to visit over here."

Hot tears blinded her eyes. She stumbled toward the door, and there collided with Elena.

Elena said softly, reproachfully to Derek, "Really, you mustn't talk that way. Stacey doesn't know you as well as we do, Derek." She took Stacey's arm. "Don't mind his moods," she went on, leading Stacey into the patio, then to the iron bench near the wall, and suggested that they sit there.

Stacey agreed, mumbled more to herself than Elena, "What did I do?"

But Elena answered, "Oh, he *does* have moods. It will be all right, I'm sure."

Alone that night, sleepless, Stacey wondered what flaw in her had made Derek turn against her. Why, wealthy and wellborn as they were, the other Alexanders were so suspicious of her. And why they tried so carefully to conceal those suspicions behind every-day good manners.

Some time during the long hours the thick silence was broken by the shrill whine of a distant car. Soon Stacey heard a long, slow, creaking sound near by.

She got up, peered out through the window. The patio was completely dark, but she could make out the faint silhouette of the open gate, a glimmer of light that quickly disappeared.

She had learned not to ask questions. She didn't mention what she had seen. It was simply one more thing for her to wonder about, among all the others.

The next morning as she left her room, she saw Derek and Maria standing together across the patio. Derek's hands were on Maria's shoulders. He was saying in a voice raised loud enough for Stacey to hear him clearly, "Now, Maria, that's enough of that. I promise you." His voice dropped. The Comanche came out of his room, carrying a load of towels. He glanced at her, repeated to Maria, "I promise you."

John came swiftly along the path. He took Stacey's arm. "Shall we go in to breakfast?" He smiled under his dark mustache, but his eyes were narrowed, suspicious.

Stacey wished he hadn't found her there, watching Derek with Maria, listening to them.

As they walked toward the dining room, John chuckled, "She's such a child, my dear. Derek had promised to buy her a trinket of some sort in town, in Piedras, that is. But he was too busy yesterday. So now . . ." John shrugged. "Now Maria is begging him not to forget again." His big hand touched Stacey in a lingering gesture.

She drew away from him quickly.

Derek had left Maria, gone on toward the main wing. Stacey hurried after him. Suddenly he stopped, not waiting for her, she realized, but listening to the sound of an approaching car.

The sound stopped abruptly. In a moment, the gate swung in. A tall man waved, then returned to the car, drove in.

"Richard," John said hoarsely.

Derek nodded. "Come on, John." And to Stacey, "Go ahead. We'll be in soon."

But she watched while Richard got out of his car. He had a typewriter in one hand, a suitcase in the other. She didn't see him again until much later in the day. She wandered around the twilight filled patio, drearily wishing the time away. She stopped at the old well, peered into its shaft which disappeared into what seemed to be the heart of the earth. She studied the straggly hollyhocks. She finally settled on the iron bench to daydream wistfully about the two beautiful months she had had with Derek.

She looked up, startled, when Richard said, "You're Derek's wife. You seemed very far away."

She very nearly told him that she wished she were far away, but managed instead to say, "And you're Richard, Derek's brother, aren't you?"

He nodded. He was lean, taller than Derek, with a hard, unsmiling mouth and cold gray eyes. Without being asked to, he sat down. "When did you come here, Stacey?"

She hesitated. It was hard to remember now. Finally, she answered, "It was the day before yesterday."

"Straight up from Mexico?"

"Yes. Through Juarez, then El Paso."

"A pleasant trip?"

She nodded, looking down to smooth her pink skirt over her knees. Taking a long breath, she said softly, "Do you want to make conversation? Or do you want to ask me a million questions?"

His low, hard voice was without inflection. "Questions are a habit with me. I'm a newspaperman, Stacey."

She had the grace to be embarrassed. She smiled at him. "I'm sorry. But the others — Elena and John — have made me feel as if I'm permanently attached to a lie detector machine."

"Have they?" he asked soberly. He got up. "I'll see you later, Stacey."

She watched him walk away, beset by an odd feeling of disappointment. For a few foolish moments, she had hoped that Richard would be her friend.

Maria came out of a room at the far end of the opposite wing, and Richard angled to meet her.

Stacey heard Maria's joyful, "Oh, Richard. You are back!" saw Richard hug Maria.

At dinner that night, she realized that he was hardly more welcome than she herself, though Stacey saw that John and Elena maintained their careful courtesy, as with her.

"Planning to be here long?" John asked.

"I don't know. I haven't decided," Richard told him.

"What about your job, Richard?" That was Elena, smiling brightly. "Can you really take off?" She turned to Stacey. "Our Richard is the only earnest Alexander. While the rest of us travel, amuse ourselves, poor Richard labors."

"I'm on a series. I'll do some of it while I'm here," Richard told her.

"I hope you'll be able to," John said doubtfully.

"Why not? I can work anywhere."

But Stacey saw that Richard was hardly listening to Elena and John. Richard's cold gray eyes moved first to Derek, then to her, slowly narrowing in bewilderment; and when Derek, as always, dismissed her from the table, Richard suddenly frowned.

The pattern set in those first few days repeated itself over the next three weeks.

One evening, returning to her room, Stacey found Maria, dressed in Stacey's clothes, preening before the mirror.

Stacey said gently, "These are mine, Maria. You oughtn't to wear them without my permission."

"Why not?" Maria demanded sullenly.

"Because they are mine."

"But a person cannot always keep to himself

what is his," Maria retorted. She pulled off Stacey's sweater, her skirt. She glided toward the door, but stopped there, for Elena stood in her way.

"Maria, what have you been doing?" Elena demanded.

"It's all right," Stacey said.

"I just wanted to see how I look in the clothes," Maria told Elena.

"Don't do it again. Now go on, Maria." Elena stepped aside, waited until Maria had hurried out, then went in to Stacey. "I'm sorry. She's such a child, isn't she?"

"I suppose she is," Stacey agreed.

"But if it happens again, you tell me." Elena nodded, paused, then asked, "Is there anything you want?"

But the thing that Stacey wanted was the thing that couldn't be named. How could she say to Elena, *I want Derek to love me again.*

One day she overheard Elena say to Derek, "You must be nicer. Don't you see what's happening?" And Derek demanded, "What does it matter? I tell you it's all right."

Stacey knew that she was the subject of their conversation, and hurried away so that she would hear no more of it.

She left the Casa de Sombra only once in those three weeks. Richard took her into Piedras for a few hours. As they drove through the gate, she asked him what the adobe bricks that stood near the wall were used for.

"Repairs." He frowned. "But I hope they don't use the pink ones. They don't belong in with the others."

Beyond the ravine, the sun was suddenly bright, reminding Stacey of Mexico. She said, smiling, "It's a lovely day."

He glanced at her. "You look like a kid let out of school early."

She didn't answer him.

He glanced at her again. "How long did you know Derek before you married him, Stacey?"

She sighed. "Oh, please, not now, Richard."

"All right. This will be an interlude." He grinned, a quick flash of white teeth in his tanned face.

"An interlude," she agreed, absurdly pleased.

Piedras was tiny, dusty, a huddled group of gasoline stations, general stores, a post office, a tiny hotel.

Richard did a few errands for Elena, bought several lengths of different colored ribbon for Maria, made some phone calls, and then insisted on buying chocolate sodas for Stacey and himself in a drug store more cluttered with goods than any Stacey had ever seen before.

They spoke of inconsequentials, and Stacey

found herself laughing, forgetting the Casa de Sombra, and yet, at the same time, she knew that Richard was watching her, studying her. On the way back, she was not surprised when he asked, "Stacey, what's wrong between you and Derek?"

"Is the interlude over, Richard?"

"I guess it is." He put a big warm hand over hers, "Tell me."

At his touch, she felt a quick leap of response in her. She snatched her hand away. "Ask Derek."

"I prefer to hear it from you."

By then, they were in the ravine again, under the shadow of the surrounding mountain ridges.

"I don't know," she said, as they drove through the cedar gates into the Casa de Sombra.

The pattern set in the first few days continued to repeat itself.

Derek treated her with polite indifference.

The Comanche, Henry, Maria stared at her through empty black eyes.

Elena and John maintained a studied politeness toward her, toward Richard, too.

And Richard was watchful, always watchful.

Many times in the night, Stacey wakened to hear the high whine of a car, to hear then the long slow squeal of the opening gate.

Many times in the dawn, she listened to the wail of an infant, a wail quickly silenced.

Unhappy, bewildered, she waited, still hoping that Derek would become himself again, the gay, laughing man that she had married.

And then, when three weeks had passed, Stacey saw Elena and Derek exchange glances over the flickering candles, and somehow in that moment, she gave up hope, surrendered her dream of love, and was filled with fear . . .

The images of memory faded from the screen of the blue velvet canopy. She sat up, clutching the quilt around her trembling body.

She understood now that Derek's love had been feigned; the impetuous courtship, the marriage — for some reason she didn't understand — a necessity to him.

That was why he became a stranger the moment they entered the Casa de Sombra. He no longer needed her.

But what had he needed her for?

Why had he pretended to love her? Why had he married her? Why had they had those two wonderful months of traveling together? Why had he brought her to the Casa de Sombra?

Like a second voice within her, fear whispered that it didn't matter. But the same second voice told her the answer.

He had needed a girl, any girl, on his trip

through Mexico, and because she had been so easily swept off her feet by his charm he had chosen her. Why? She pictured herself wearing the huge orchids he had bought her, pictured him bending to kiss her, remembered waving as they drove past the border customs officials like joyful honeymooners. Derek had smuggled something, what, she didn't know or care, into the country. Elena and John knew about it. That was why they were so suspicious of her.

She sat up slowly. She was sure, sure.

Derek didn't love her, never had, never would.

And she? She wondered if she had ever truly loved him.

She slipped off the bed, folded the quilt, put it carefully aside. She brushed her hair, put on lipstick. Her wide blue eyes were shiny with held-back tears. Her heart beat in quick blows against her ribs.

She knew what she must do.

She had to find Derek, tell him that she was leaving him, leaving the house of shadow forever.

Chapter Four

She turned off the lights in her room. She stood at the door, listening. She tried not to think of all those things she dared not say. Above all, she had to perpetuate for Derek, for Elena and John and Richard, the image of her ignorance. If she admitted that she knew the truth, they might never allow her to leave.

There were no sounds from outside. She eased the heavy door open, stepped into the darkness. She waited, holding her breath, but the silence was thick, heavy.

Then she hurried along the path, ran across the patio, afraid to be found there, afraid that she would lose her courage.

Derek's window was dark. There was no light showing at the half-open door. She pushed it in, called his name, but the room was empty, still.

There was a sudden sound from somewhere behind her. She turned. Across the patio near her room, she saw a gliding shadow drift into concealing darkness.

She ran back to her room.

The door was open, though she knew that she had closed it carefully only moments before.

She was afraid to move, but she had to go in, to know, to see. She forced herself across the threshold. Nothing moved in the darkness. She found the light, turned it on.

Maria lay on the bed. Maria, crushed, small, limp, her arms flung wide, a dark red stain between her shoulder blades.

Stacey went to her, touched her, felt the warmth of blood, and knew death when she saw it.

A scream built up in Stacey's throat and ripped the fabric of the night as she turned to flee and blundered into Elena who barred the door, demanding, "Stacey, what's the matter?"

"Maria. On the bed . . . she's . . . I'm afraid she's dead."

Then John, Derek, Richard, together, crowded in, and the room was full of confusion.

Stacey crouched against the wall, numb with shock.

Richard, kneeling beside Maria, whispered, "Poor kid, why did it have to happen to you?" And touched her cheek gently, and then looking at the floor, "Yes. The knife is here."

The others had been talking, exchanging questions, answers. Now they were silent. They turned speculative eyes on Stacey.

She said, "I went out. For just a minute,

I think, and when I came back she was here. Like that."

"You mean you found her here?" Elena asked. "Is that what you're trying to tell us? You found her here dead?

"There's blood on your hands, Stacey," Elena told her.

Stacey looked at her trembling fingers. They were a wet greasy red. She rubbed them on her skirt, leaving long dark streaks.

John said soberly, "I do believe there's fire in Stacey after all."

"Be quiet, John." Richard came to stand beside Stacey. "You'd better get Bill Abel and his bunch up from Piedras." Richard explained to Stacey. "He's the sheriff."

"Stacey," Elena asked. "You said you went out. Where did you go?"

"To Derek's room. But he wasn't there." She looked at Derek questioningly. He ignored her.

Elena said softly, "You found Maria trying on your clothes once, didn't you? And then earlier tonight she was wearing your little white hat when you came in. Did you want her out of the way, Stacey?"

Stacey gasped, "No. No, Elena. I didn't . . . I didn't touch Maria. I . . ." Her voice trailed away. She stared first at Elena, then at Derek.

She thought that she must have all along suspected that there was something between Derek and Maria. But now with Elena's words, it had become clear. Maria had tried to drive Stacey away, had said, "This is a bad house. You will not be happy here." She had said, "You are not hurt. I am." Maria and Derek had been lovers once, perhaps continued to be after Derek brought Stacey home with him.

"I'll get Bill," John said.

"Tell Henry and The Comanche," Richard added, and waved John out of the room.

Elena leaned against the wall. "So you were jealous of her."

"No," Stacey cried. "I had no reason. I didn't know . . ."

But no one answered her.

Henry, his face gray, stumbled in, holding The Comanche. Together they knelt beside Maria's still body.

They made a soft sound of grief, a keening that was like a song, a sad and terrible sound.

Richard said, "Don't touch her, Henry."

Derek and Elena exchanged a glance. "There are a lot of other things to do," Elena said. "You'd better take care of them, Derek."

He nodded, went out.

The Comanche raised her head, demanded, "Why did she die? Eighteen. Eighteen is too young to die."

"Be quiet now," Elena told her. "Either you'll be quiet or you'll have to leave her."

Stacey whispered, "I'll go out into the air for a minute. I . . ."

But Elena said silkily, "Oh, no. I think you'd better not."

"But I didn't do it," Stacey cried. "You know that I didn't!"

"I *know* it?" Elena shrugged. "I'm afraid we'll have to wait and see, won't we?" Then added, "But who else would possibly have anything against Maria?"

The Comanche and Henry suddenly raised their heads. No longer impassive, their swarthy faces were full of hate.

"We don't know anything yet," Richard said.

And Stacey asked herself who could have wanted to see Maria dead. Who but Derek — Derek, whose room had been empty when she went there to see him. She had seen a gliding shadow disappear into the patio gloom near her door. Could it have been Derek? She wasn't sure. She didn't know. But why should Derek have killed Maria? If they had been lovers, Stacey had only just realized it. She was in no way a threat to their affair. Nor was Maria a threat to anyone. Why then had Maria died?

Stacey shivered. Could she have been infatuated with a man who was willing to murder an eighteen-year-old girl? Could she have married such a man?

Confused, she whispered, "It's like a terrible dream."

"Who would have thought such a thing could happen here, in our family."

"A terrible dream. All of it. From beginning to end," Stacey whispered. "Since the moment we passed the gate . . . since we came . . ." Her voice broke. "And I can't wake up."

"You will soon enough," Elena told her.

In a low hard voice Richard said, "That will do, Elena."

Suddenly the room was full of men, uniforms, guns, deep voices.

Stacey huddled against the wall, alone, waiting.

The threat, the danger, that she had sensed earlier that night had become real.

Chapter Five

The living room was warm, bright. White walls were hung with brightly-colored woven serapes and brass trays. A huge bank of cactus in pots was under the velvet-draped window.

Stacey listened dully to the talk that swirled around her. She crouched in a big chair, wide-eyed, knowing that a web of danger drew tighter and tighter around her.

The others — Bill Abel, the sheriff; and Jed Lincoln, his deputy; and the Alexanders — were old friends. That was obvious in the way Bill asked Richard, "Well, how are things going down in Albuquerque?" and teased Elena about her high-speed driving, and thanked Derek for the postcard mailed him from Mexico.

Only Stacey was the outsider.

Bill Abel was a big man, very blond, with tanned, weathered skin, and narrowed blue eyes. His voice was quiet, almost a whisper. He sighed, said finally, "Well, the state boys have done their jobs, and the coroner's about to do his. So I better get down to mine." He looked at Stacey, "You want to tell me what happened?"

She licked her dry lips. She folded her

trembling hands in her lap. "I had to talk to Derek. I went across the patio to his room."

"You have your own then. Married two months, plus three weeks, and you've got your own room?"

Her cheeks burned. She nodded. "Yes, you see . . ."

"Sure. I see," Bill said.

But it was plain to Stacey that he didn't. He thought she had sent Derek away from her.

"Go on," he told her, his whispery voice somehow more threatening than if he had shouted.

"It was dark. The door was ajar. Nobody was there."

"Why did you want to see him?"

"To talk to him."

"In the middle of the night? Was it urgent?"

"It wasn't that late."

"What did you want to talk about?"

"I wanted to . . ."

But Richard cut in, "What difference does that make?"

Bill shot him a narrow blue look, turned back to Stacey. "All right. Then?"

"I went back to my room. I'd closed the door when I left, but it was open. I went in, turned on the light. Maria was there. On the bed."

"You've got blood all over you," Bill said.

"I touched her. I wanted to see . . ." Stacey swallowed. "I screamed. And Elena, the others, came in."

"Stacey," Elena asked gently, "was she trying on your things again? Is that what happened?"

Stacey shook her head. "No. And that didn't matter anyway."

"You want to get it off your chest now?" Bill asked. "Tell me how it was?"

Derek leaned against the wall, his dark eyes thoughtful.

"I didn't kill Maria," Stacey cried. "I just wanted to tell Derek that I . . ."

"Yes?" Bill whispered.

"That I . . . that I was going to leave him."

The silence was thick, stifling.

Stacey knew she had made a mistake. She shouldn't have said that, not without first having told Derek. She should have waited. Because she couldn't, she didn't dare give her true reason. Their marriage had been a lie. He had used her when he needed her to cover something he had done. She somehow connected it with smuggling, but she didn't dare say so.

Elena cried, shocked, "But Stacey, you couldn't have thought that Maria and Derek . . ."

It was in that way, subtly, indirectly, with apparent unwillingness, that she put the motive into Bill Abel's mind.

"You got the idea that there was something between Maria and Derek?"

Jed Lincoln, the deputy, moved restlessly. He was short, round. The pistol on his belt looked like a toy against the bulk of his hip.

"Well?" Bill demanded.

"I didn't know. That didn't matter either," she said at last.

John, silent until then, asked, "What about the knife, Bill?"

"There's nothing on the hilt and not likely to be," Bill said. "It's one of those from the cabinet in the dining room. I recognize it myself."

Henry came in with coffee, served it.

The men leaned back, lit cigarettes.

There was a brief social moment, strangely out of place it seemed to Stacey, then Bill looked at her. "You know the knives, don't you?"

She remembered noticing them the first day she had come, when she had dropped her ring under the breakfront. She nodded. "But I never touched them." She paused. "I wasn't in my room. Don't you see? I couldn't have done it."

"And before you went out?" Bill asked.

"No!" Stacey cried.

"You found her there, didn't you? And you had the knife. And after you'd stabbed her, just lost your head probably, not meaning to kill her, then you went over to Derek's room, hoping he'd help you, maybe . . ."

The web of danger tightened, noose-like, around Stacey. She shivered uncontrollably. Desperate for help, she looked at Derek.

Richard rose. He set his coffee cup on a marble-topped table. He said harshly, "This has gone as far as it's going to go. Stacey is a sweet little girl and surprisingly innocent in some ways." He gave her a quick, hard, warning look. "Since she's not going to tell you, I will. We were together. I was with her. I was — not Maria. When Stacey went to talk to Derek, I saw her cross the patio, stop at Derek's door. I went to my room. Maria came to Stacey's room, was killed there while Stacey was across the patio. Look further." He gave Bill a hard grin. "Sorry."

There was a brief silence.

"But when she came back . . . Suppose Maria was there then. Stacey did it, then screamed."

"The knife," Richard said. "She had no time to get the knife."

"Earlier," Bill snapped.

"Sorry again." Richard's hard grin came

once more. "Earlier I noticed that all the knives were in the cabinet where they belonged. That was after Stacey left the dining room. The three of us remained, so she couldn't have gone back to get it."

"But Richard," Stacey protested. "What are you saying? You know . . ."

"Quiet, Stacey. I don't care if Derek gets the wrong idea. This is too important."

Bill Abel sighed, got to his feet. "I thought this was going to be easy."

"But aren't you going to do anything?" Elena demanded.

"Sure. Soon. We'll be back." Bill gave Stacey a narrowed blue look. "And if I were you, I'd stay put. I wouldn't try to run away."

"Why should she?" Richard demanded.

"You're gallant, hunh? I never knew that, Richard." Bill took up his big hat, nodded at Jed Lincoln. "We'll let you know about the inquest and all that."

When the policeman had gone, Derek said softly, "Poor Stacey, why did you do it?"

"I didn't," she whispered. "You know I didn't!"

And she remembered his empty room, the shadow gliding away from her room as she turned to go back to it. She hadn't killed Maria, she knew. But Derek . . . Derek might have.

Chapter Six

The desk was big. Its top littered with sheets of paper, pencils, cigarette ash. The typewriter sat uncovered on its center. It was obviously a place of work. The rest of the room was neat, well-lived in, and disciplined.

"I think you'll be comfortable here," Richard said. "Anyhow, for tonight it's better."

She said quickly, "Yes, thanks, Richard. I'm glad you suggested we change."

"You look as if you could do with some rest."

"And Richard, thanks for saying I was with you. Though I don't know why you did, nor even how it will help. Nor . . ."

"Smoke screen."

"What?"

"Bill Abel's not stupid, but not brilliant either. A small diversion might help."

"But why, Richard? Why should he think I did it?" She knew the answer to that as soon as she asked it. She was the outsider. She had been planning to leave Derek. Elena, without directly accusing her, had suggested a motive to Bill. "Why don't you?"

Richard said, "Let's say I don't believe you're handy with knives. Are you?"

"Richard!"

"No. Of course not."

"The rest of them — Elena, Derek, John — they all want to believe it though." She stared at Richard. "But you lied for me."

"I saw him making up his mind."

"But when he finds out the lie?"

"He can't. I was here. Nobody saw me. If I say I was with you until you left your room, I was with you," he said harshly. "Now do you understand?"

"We alibi each other," she said slowly.

He nodded.

Why had he helped her, she asked herself suddenly. Was it for her? Or for himself? She remembered suddenly how Maria had greeted him on his arrival, warmly, joyfully; how he had bought her ribbons in Piedras. Could there have been something between Maria and him?

She shrugged the ugly suspicion away.

But he seemed to have read her thoughts. He said, "You *do* understand."

She didn't answer him. She was seeing the room again — Maria dead — the bed, the quilt, stained with blood.

As soon as the police had left, Richard had suggested that she take his room for the night. He had walked her across the patio so that she could pick up a gown, a robe. Then he had brought her here.

It was the final astonishment, capping the whole evening. He, rather than Derek, had known she couldn't sleep on the bed where Maria had breathed her last. He had cared.

And now, having lied to protect her, he admitted that the same lie protected him.

"Stacey," he asked, "when did you meet Derek?"

"I've told you. In Mexico City. Two months, three weeks ago."

"It's true then?"

"Yes."

"And married him. Just like that. It seems an odd thing for a girl like you to do. If you had no reason, that is."

"I had one. Then."

"What?" he asked quickly.

"I thought I was in love."

"Thought?"

His cold gray eyes studied her, judged her, weighed her.

She didn't answer him. Instead, she whispered, "Richard, do you know why Derek married me?"

"I wouldn't dwell on that too much, Stacey."

She didn't trust him. There were too many questions in her mind. She didn't dare tell him about the strange towns she and Derek had visited, the odd people he had talked to, the nights he had left her and gone walking alone. She was afraid to describe their border crossing. Had Derek's reason for marrying her been connected with Maria's death?

"She was a good kid, Maria," Richard said. "It shouldn't have ended like this." He nodded at Stacey. "Get some sleep now," and went out.

Alone, she sank down on the bed. She rubbed her eyes wearily.

It seemed an age since she had decided to tell Derek she was leaving him. But it was only a few hours since she had realized that he didn't love her, never had and never would. And that she, mistaking infatuation for love, had made the grotesque error which led her to the house of shadow, to disillusion, to fear.

The room with Richard gone seemed strangely cold, empty.

She undressed, put on her gown, slipped into bed. She huddled under the maroon quilt, her eyes closed against the light that she had not dared put out.

Someone had killed Maria. Who? Who had hated her so? Why?

Was it connected with Derek's reason for marrying Stacey? Elena and John were involved in Derek's plot, whatever it was. The bits and pieces of conversation that Stacey had heard could make sense only if Derek's sister and brother *were* involved. Their barely-concealed suspicions, resentment of her proved that. And Elena, the dominant member of the family, had seemed, indirectly, to call Bill Abel's attention to Stacey.

How could she find out the truth, she asked herself.

How?

Dawn slowly edged the window, and some time just before she drifted off into uneasy sleep, she heard an infant cry.

Chapter Seven

Stacey looked in bewilderment from face to face, searching for a sign, a faint indication that the night before had left a trail in their memories. But the Alexanders seemed to have been untouched, unmarked. It was as if nothing had happened.

John licked marmalade off the edge of his mustache and asked The Comanche for more coffee.

Richard thoughtfully buttered a piece of toast.

Elena sipped orange juice.

Derek carefully cracked his soft-boiled eggs.

Stacey wondered if it were all a horrible dream, a dream that she alone had had. Only she, alone, isolated from the others by a barrier of fear, seemed to remember.

Murder had been done, but they were unaffected. Death was in the house, but they were untouched.

She glanced at Richard again. It was hard to read his stony face, his gray eyes. Perhaps that lack of expression covered feeling. He had liked Maria, been kind to her. Stacey thought of the alibi he had given both of them, wondered which of them it actually protected.

Then John said, "Stacey, my dear, Bill called a few minutes ago. He is on his way out here. He'll want to question you."

She nodded.

"He asked that I remind you you aren't to leave."

"But I couldn't. Why would I? Not until we know who killed Maria."

Elena looked at John, asked, "Did you take care of everything?"

"Yes, I did."

"Everything?" Derek asked.

"Of course."

"I've made the arrangements for Henry and The Comanche," Richard said.

"Yes." Elena slanted a glance at him. "I intended to ask if you would. We do have some obligations after all."

"They'll go into Piedras after breakfast. Bill said it would be all right by then. I guess they'll be back by dinner time."

"Good." Elena nodded. "Life goes on. And I wish that Bill would get the rest of it over with."

"He will," John soothed her. "We all know Bill."

So Stacey knew it was no dream. Maria had been murdered. And Stacey herself, the stranger in the Casa de Sombra, would have to prove her innocence. But how?

Bill Abel, with Jed, settled down in the living room. He saw the Alexanders one by one. Stacey was the last to be called, and waited, knowing that being kept for last had a special significance.

At last, when it was her turn, she sat in the chair toward which Bill gestured.

Richard tried to stay with her, but Bill refused.

"It's her right to have somebody," Richard insisted.

"Her right?" Bill's pale brows rose. "What right? All I'm doing is asking questions. She's got no rights. No more than anybody else." After Richard had left them, Bill turned to Stacey, demanded, "You worried about your rights?"

"I just want to tell the truth." But she remembered the lie Richard had told, the lie she had allowed to stand. Her cheeks burned. She twisted her small hands in her lap, said earnestly, "Sheriff, I didn't kill Maria."

"You didn't." His voice was a flat, uninterested whisper. "But you were jealous of Maria, weren't you? Even to the point of threatening to leave Derek. That gives you a motive. Nobody else had one."

Stacey wondered if Elena, in her careful way, had strengthened Bill's ideas even more, had somehow managed to cast heavier suspicion on her.

She said, "There's another explanation, I know."

Bill ignored that. "Now, I want your full name, and where you were born, and when, and . . ."

She answered the avalanche of questions, slowly, carefully, truthfully. Truthfully, until Bill worked his way to those moments when she had been alone before going to see Derek. Then — ashamed, not wanting to, but afraid not to — she confirmed what Richard had said. Not for him, but for herself. With that thought, she shuddered. Could Richard have stabbed Maria? Or Derek? Or . . . ?

Bill studied her, went on, his whisper more menacing than ever. Questions, more questions. Old ones. New ones.

Stacey's head ached. Her eyes burned.

Suddenly, it was over. Bill demanded, "Do you want to stick with what you've told me? You and Richard were together. You left him, went to see Derek. When you came back to your room, you found Maria there, dead?"

"That's how it was."

Bill looked at Jed. "Get them all in here."

When the others had joined them, Bill said, "This is how it is. Maria must have been killed just before Stacey found her and screamed, or it happened while she was in Derek's room. Earlier Richard and Stacey were together. Stacey didn't have a chance to get the knife. Right?"

"*If* the two of them were together," Derek said thoughtfully.

"Can you prove we weren't?" Richard demanded.

"Why should I?" Derek shrugged. "I was taking a walk." He grinned at Bill. "Alone, as I've told you."

Her voice full of reproach, Elena murmured, "Why Bill, after all these questions! How could any of us have done it?"

"I got to ask, don't I?" He looked at Stacey. "You sure you screamed as soon as you saw her?"

"She screamed the second she stepped into the room," Richard said. "I was at the window. I know. The light went on and she screamed."

"You didn't say that last night," Derek told him.

"Bill didn't ask about that last night," Richard retorted.

Bill sighed. "Which leaves us back where we were." He looked at Stacey. "I'll be back. You be around."

Chapter Eight

She waited until the others had gone.

Those few moments gave her time to regain strength, regain her breath, to control the terror which ticked away inside of her, a bomb ready to explode and destroy her forever.

When she was calmer, more sure of her self-control, she went in search of Derek. She found him at the foot of the patio, sitting on the pile of tan and pink adobe bricks.

She stood before him, her hands in the pockets of her skirt, sandy head bent, hair shining in spite of the shadow over the patio. "Derek, tell me, why did you marry me? Why did you have to?"

"Have to?" He grinned. "What an odd way to put it. What a strange question to ask."

"You never loved me, Derek."

"We're married. You're my wife." He grinned again. "And I don't appreciate your having invited Richard into your bedroom either."

"I didn't . . ." she said hotly.

The admission hung between them, spoken, stressed, no longer retractable.

"Oh?" Derek laughed. "I suspected as much. As you know."

"That doesn't matter, Derek."

"Bill Abel will certainly think that a very important lie."

She put out her hand, a small involuntary gesture. "Derek, tell me. What did you want? Why did you bring me here? Does it have anything to do with Maria's death?"

"I brought you because it seemed a good idea." He paused, added, "If I were you, I'd be worrying about my skin. Not asking stupid questions."

"You weren't in your room, Derek. Were you with Maria?"

"I told Bill. I was out walking."

"She loved you, didn't she, Derek? That was what it was all about — why she hated me — why she tried on my clothes. She wanted to be me, wanted to be your wife."

"What an admirable imagination," he said. He rose from the adobe brick pile, brushed pink and tan dust from his blue trousers, and walked away.

She went back to her room, stayed there, alone, again, thinking.

What an imagination you have, he had said. The same words as the time she asked him about the infant's cry.

The high whine of a car nearby, a car in the night at the gate. The low thin sound of iron hinges opening. The faint glimmer of a flash, quickly gone. How many times had she listened, wakeful and alone, to those sounds? To those sounds, and the infant's cry? And Derek had said she had a strong imagination.

The Comanche, stony-faced, called her at dinner time.

Pausing outside the dining room, Stacey heard raised voices, stopped to listen.

"It's all your fault, Derek," Elena cried, her low musical voice suddenly shrill. "We'd have been through, home free, traveling in the Orient by now, except for your stupidity."

"I couldn't help it, Elena. That's just how it was. I had to do something, and I did."

"But don't you see . . . now . . ."

There was a touch on her shoulder. Stacey cringed, a swift hot current of fright rushing through her.

His eyes cold, Richard said, "It's about time to go in, isn't it?"

She expected that the police would return. She had waited for them since after breakfast, rehearsing in her mind what she would say to them.

It would require candor, an exposure of herself, which she dreaded. Yet she knew that only by giving Bill Abel the truth, and all of it, could she hope to convince him that Maria's murder, Stacey's own arrival, the strangeness of her marriage, were all related.

She had to explain that Derek had married her because he needed a cover; something, she didn't know what exactly, that had to do, perhaps with smuggling. She must describe their two months trip, and then describe, no matter how it embarrassed her, the change in Derek as soon as they arrived at the Casa de Sombra. She must tell Bill Abel about the conversations between Elena and Derek that Stacey had overheard — all those fragments which added up to only one thing. The Alexanders did not want Stacey in the Casa de Sombra, but were afraid to have her leave. Stacey had to tell about the sounds in the night, the infant crying; explain why she had been going to leave Derek. And having said all that, she must also confess that Richard had lied. He had not been with her during the time she left the dining room and went to talk to Derek. Once Bill knew all of the truth, he must believe that she knew nothing — nothing of Maria's death.

Stacey waited, expecting a summons to the living room any time, going over it in her mind. By late afternoon the sheriff had not yet appeared.

She went out into the patio.

Richard was sitting on the bench near the well. He looked at her, called to her.

She went to sit beside him, realizing suddenly that she must warn him she was going to tell Bill the truth. She took a deep breath. "This morning, Richard, I told Derek that you weren't with me."

Richard gave her an amused look. "You couldn't bear to have him think the wrong thing?"

"It wasn't that," she cried. "It just slipped out, and then I had to explain. But I am going to tell Bill Abel anyhow."

"You are?"

"I have to, Richard."

"You'd have done better to keep your mouth shut, Stacey."

"Better for your sake, or for mine?" she demanded.

"What do you think?"

"I don't know."

"That's wise," he said, his voice hard. "Don't trust anybody. And even more important, don't think too much." He looked into her face, his expression unreadable. He reached out, patted her cheek.

His fingers were warm, gentle, oddly comforting. She remembered suddenly, though, that he had once patted Maria's cheek. Stacey shrank away.

He got up, walked away, without a word.

She was relieved that he had left her, yet sorry, too.

A breeze shifted the well rope, causing the big iron bucket to clang against the wall.

Derek suddenly leaned over her. "You were miles away in your thoughts, weren't you, darling?"

She stared at him.

"But here you are in Casa de Sombra with me."

"Until the police discover the truth," she said.

"Forever, Stacey."

"Don't be ridiculous, Derek."

"You *are* my wife."

"That can be changed, and will be," she said softly.

"Poor darling, you don't understand men, do you?" Derek's dark eyes shone with amusement. "I'm sorry if I hurt you in these past weeks. But it's over now. I'll have your things moved to my room tonight."

"Don't bother," she said coldly, "because I won't move with them."

She was surprised at the depth of loathing she suddenly felt for him. How had she ever believed that she loved him? How had she ever allowed herself to be deceived by him?

Now it was so easy to understand him, see through him. This new gambit was part of everything that had happened. Perhaps it had been suggested by one of the other Alexanders. Stacey must be kept in the Casa de Sombra now. She knew too many of its secrets, and they knew that she knew them. She must be kept in the Casa de Sombra until . . .

A hand seemed to squeeze her heart. She looked away from Derek's smiling face toward the mountain ridges.

Derek said softly, "If you're wise, you may some day leave here."

It was, very clearly, a threat. She didn't answer him.

There was the sound of a car. The huge gate swung open.

Stacey straightened up in quick relief. She expected it to be Bill Abel and Jed Lincoln. Instead, an old car rattled into the patio. When it stopped, Henry got out. He walked stiffly back to the gate, swung it shut. The Comanche waited until he joined her, then the two of them, bowed figures carrying bouquets of flowers, went into the house.

"The funeral is over then."

"The funeral? Derek! No one from the family went."

Derek shrugged. "We have other things on our minds, I'm afraid."

"You're heartless," she whispered.

"Remember that when you speak to Bill Abel," he said.

"You want him to arrest me, don't you?

So that you'll be safely rid of me."

"You're more clever than I thought." He gave an exaggerated sigh. "Elena and John are right, I guess."

"But don't you see?" Stacey pleaded. "I don't really understand. And I don't care. I just want to leave here."

Derek said, "Any ideas you do have, you'd better keep to yourself. If you don't, I assure you, you'll regret it." He left her then.

She waited until he had disappeared into his room, thinking over his admission that he and the others wanted to see her arrested, taken away. She wondered why he had spoken so freely to her.

But she couldn't understand it. Finally, she rose, went toward the wing where The Comanche and Henry had their room.

As she approached it, Henry came out, closed the door carefully, and walked stiffly to meet her.

"I'm sorry about Maria," she said. "You do know that, don't you?"

He nodded.

"I wasn't told about the funeral, Henry. Explain it to The Comanche for me."

He nodded again.

She whispered, "Henry, I didn't kill Maria. Please, please, you must believe me."

A ripple of expression moved across his usually impassive face, then faded. "We know," he said quietly.

"Do you know who did?"

Without having moved, he seemed to edge her away from the door. He turned, and his black eyes focused far away on the mountain ridges, dyed now with the brilliant colors of sunset. "We do not know," he said at last.

The door of the room suddenly snapped open. The Comanche peered out. She called out a staccato Spanish sentence. Henry looked at Stacey, hesitated, then went to The Comanche. They whispered together briefly, looked at Stacey from blank black eyes, and disappeared inside.

Stacey went back to her room.

Why had Maria been killed? she asked herself.

Who had done it?

How could she convince Bill Abel of her innocence?

How could she leave the Casa de Sombra, escape the shadow that lay over it, escape the menace that surrounded her?

She waited, hoping that the sheriff would come. But he didn't.

The family gathered for dinner, silent, abstracted.

Stacey was relieved when Derek said, at last, "You can go to your room, if you're finished."

The evening passed slowly.
She was alone with her frightened thoughts.
Finally, she fell asleep.

Chapter Nine

She was dreaming. A church bell tolled. Its sweet, sad sound spilled over the countryside. She wakened suddenly, sat up.

Gray dawn filled the room.

It was empty, still.

Nothing but gray dawn, and . . . ?

She slipped out of bed, drew on her robe.

A cold wind enwrapped her when she opened the door. She peered into the patio. It, too, was empty and still, except for the whispering of the moving hollyhocks, the creak of the well rope.

She stared at it, her eyes widening.

Something dangled at the rope. Something large, heavy; it moved, swayed.

Watching it, she whimpered. She took a step, then another toward it. She was drawn there on unwilling feet, drawn closer, until once again caught in a nightmare, she screamed.

Derek was waiting for her. He waited, his dark head at an odd angle — his feet, moving in the air inches above the well wall. He waited, hanging in the noose of the old rope, his face swollen, twisted, his eyes bulging . . .

She screamed and screamed again, and the

gray gloom of the patio was suddenly streaked with light. The silence broke with sound.

Footsteps came pounding toward her. She ran to meet them.

Richard cried, "Stacey . . . Stacey . . ." and opened his arms to her, and she crumpled against him.

First Maria.

Then Derek.

That was all Stacey could think of.

Elena had stopped weeping now. Her face was pale and swollen but composed, as she sat beside John, clinging to his plump hand.

Richard silently paced the floor.

Bill Abel leaned back in his chair, blue eyes squinting at the silver coffee urn. "If there's more of that, I could stand some."

Richard filled a cup for him, for Jed Lincoln.

Bill nodded his thanks, sighed. "It's been quite a morning."

"For all of us," John said grimly.

"Yes," Bill agreed, looking at Stacey.

She shrank under that speculative stare.

"I can tell you what I know," Bill went on. "Derek was hit on the head. The mark is plain. There's an adobe brick from the pile at the gate, I'd guess." Bill sipped coffee. "That brick is right there, near the well. He got hit and knocked out. The top was tied around him. That big old bucket went into the well, and . . ."

His words hung in the still air.

Elena gasped.

Stacey whispered, "The bucket hitting the side of the well, going down . . . that's what I heard."

"Maybe that's what you heard," Bill said. "Maybe you heard it from right beside him, too."

"No!" she cried.

Elena spoke suddenly, her voice brittle, "If that's how it happened, then a woman *could* have done it."

It was out in the open. Elena's enmity was no longer a subtle thing, but spoken, clear, direct.

"No!" Stacey cried again.

Elena turned, eyes suddenly aflame with hate. "Stacey, you told us all that you were going to leave him. He objected, didn't he? The Alexanders have never had a divorce. Derek wouldn't allow it."

Bill Abel said, "You *were* going to leave him."

That was the moment for her to tell him the truth of everything that had happened. She drew a long slow breath, prepared herself.

But Richard cut in smoothly, "Elena, I'm afraid you're distraught."

"You should rest, Elena," John told her, stroking his mustache.

But all of them, all of the Alexanders, were staring at Stacey; and she found that she couldn't speak — not then — with them watching her.

She was simply gagged by fear.

Bill shook his head. "I never had anything like this before."

"You're in over your head," Richard told him "Call in the state police."

Bill got up, retorted, "You newspaper guys are all alike. You want miracles. It's only been a couple of hours. What do you expect?"

"Answers. That's not asking for too much."

Elena was suddenly controlled again. "We know so little of Stacey," she said softly. "Perhaps . . . I'm sorry, Stacey, dear, but perhaps there's some odd strain in her. Perhaps she's . . ."

All eyes turned to Stacey. Under the weight of those watchful stares, she shrank back.

"That's a thought," Bill grumbled. "Only it isn't proof. What I need is proof."

John smiled gently at Stacey, "You needn't worry, you know. We're your family. We'll stand by you."

"Let's go," Bill told Jed Lincoln. "We've got things to do in town."

"But what about what's happened here?"

John demanded.

"We'll have to wait for the autopsy no matter what," Bill answered. He glared at Richard, "The state police do that."

Stacey got to her feet. "'Take me with you, please.'"

"What?" Bill swung on her. "You decide to confess?"

"I have nothing to confess," she said steadily.

"Be quiet," Richard said softly, coming to stand beside her.

"I can't stay here," she told Bill. "Arrest me. Keep me in jail, until you know the truth."

John chuckled, "Why, maybe Elena's got a point after all. If you're innocent, why should you go to jail, Stacey?"

"I'm afraid. I'm afraid to stay here," she cried.

Elena got to her feet. "You have nothing to be afraid of."

Bill demanded, "What about it?"

Elena laughed softly, appealingly, "You see, Bill?"

"Something will happen," Stacey cried. "I know it. I feel it."

He sighed. "I can't arrest you without proof, Stacey. You think about it. If you confess, why okay . . ." He shrugged, "But if you don't . . ."

She wanted to scream, "Yes, yes, I did it. I killed them both. Just take me away from here." To say anything that would get her out of the Casa de Sombra. But she didn't dare. If she once said those words, she knew she would be saddled with them forever. No one would believe her when she retracted them. And some time, somehow, she would have to retract them, or she would be judged a murderess.

"Well?" Bill was asking.

She shook her head.

"I'll be back," he told her. "We'll get it settled."

She knew he was almost convinced of her guilt. It was in the look he gave her before he and Jed Lincoln left.

When they were alone, Elena sank into the sofa again. "I can't believe it," she whispered. "Derek gone."

"We have a lot to do," John said.

"Yes. Yes. And quickly, too." She turned her head, stared steadily at Stacey. "I hope you'll forgive me. Perhaps I did lose my head. But it's Derek, you see . . . and . . ."

"And as I told you before, Stacey, my dear," John cut in, "we are your family. You have nothing to fear from us, you know."

She looked at him, wide-eyed.

"It's true," he insisted.

Elena whispered, "I shouldn't have blamed you, Stacey. It's only . . . well, we've always lived such quiet lives. And since you've come here . . ."

Stacey stared at Elena, at John.

Elena had first subtly accused her of murdering Maria, then overtly accused her of murdering Derek. Now, suddenly, they were trying to make amends for that.

And she knew why. They wanted her to remain in the Casa de Sombra. They didn't want her to leave, not now, not yet, perhaps never.

She got to her feet.

"Where are you going?" Elena demanded.

"To my room," Stacey said.

When she went out, Richard went with her.

"Do you insist on sticking your head into the lion's mouth?" he demanded.

"I don't know what you mean."

He took her hand. "Stacey, you must realize that you're in danger."

"Yes, I do," she whispered.

"Do you? Then why did you ask Bill Abel to take you away? It was an open confession of your suspicions, you know."

"I couldn't help it, Richard. I'm afraid." She gave him a faint smile. "And between Bill and the family, I'll take Bill."

"That might not be wise."

"I don't know any more."

He let go of her hand. "I think you know more than you should."

"What do you mean, Richard?"

He ignored her question. "Why didn't you tell Bill everything?"

"Everything?"

"About the alibi I gave you," Richard said gently.

"I don't know. I was frightened. I couldn't think, I suppose."

His voice was suddenly very soft. "Stacey, do you have friends, anyone to help you now?"

"I'm completely alone."

"Now would be the time to call on them."

"If only there were someone," she said bitterly. "When I married, I thought . . ."

But she didn't go on. There was no use to speak — to even think about those sweet hopes that had died in the Casa de Sombra.

"Since you haven't told Bill yet about the night Maria died, I suggest you don't, Stacey. At least not now. That's the best advice I can give you for the moment."

She didn't answer him. They were at the door of her room. She paused there.

"I wish you had never come here, Stacey," he said quietly.

"So do I," she whispered. Then she went in.

Chapter Ten

The day passed slowly, dimly.

Stacey sat alone in her room, staring at the blank walls, asking herself unanswerable questions.

What was the plot in which all the Alexanders, including Derek, were involved?

What had Elena and John feared she might know that Derek was certain she didn't know? It had to be that — Derek against the other two. They had masked their suspicions, their resentment of her. Only Derek had been himself, natural to her, as soon as they arrived at the Casa de Sombra.

Could Maria have known something? Could Derek, Elena, John, even Richard have silenced her because she was a threat to them?

Then why had Derek become the next victim?

Stacey's thoughts were interrupted by Elena.

The tall, dark-haired woman came in with The Comanche, bringing a tray.

The small stout Indian gave Stacey a blank look, turned and waddled out.

Elena sat on the edge of the bed, smoothed her black riding trousers. "The funeral will be tomorrow. Ten o'clock, Stacey."

Stacey nodded.

"Do you have black?"

"Yes. A skirt and blouse."

"Good." Then, "I know you don't feel much grief, but still . . ."

"I have feelings, Elena," Stacey said softly. "And . . . and I have a few memories, too." Her throat was tight, the words strained.

"Yes. That wasn't necessary. I oughtn't to have said it." Elena paused. Then, "We're a family. It's like John said. I'm glad you planned to go with us."

"Of course I'd go with you. There's no reason why I shouldn't."

"It's best that way," Elena said. She went to the door. "I'm sorry."

The insincere words seemed to echo in the room after she had gone.

Stacey knew there was some purpose to Elena's behavior. It could only be that Elena believed Stacey knew something — something about the Casa de Sombra, about Derek, about all the Alexanders — that must be concealed. But if that were true, Stacey thought, she herself didn't know what it could be.

She had no more than faint hints, glimmerings.

Derek had married her for some special reason, brought her home with him. She had thought he might be smuggling something into the country. But she had no proof of that. None. Only the strangeness of their trip, only the way he changed once they reached the house, only those sounds in the night which no one but she herself had ever admitted hearing.

Why had Elena and John — and yes, even Richard — been so much against her from the moment they saw her? It could only be because they thought they had some reason to distrust her. But what reason?

And why had Maria been murdered?

Why Derek?

Confused, more frightened than ever, she wondered if there was a madman in the Casa de Sombra — if, as Elena had suggested about Stacey herself, someone hid a sickness behind an everyday mask, a sickness which had driven him to kill?

Was it John?

Elena?

Stacey's thoughts paused, her mind a resistant blank. But then she forced herself to go on. Was it Richard?

She found it difficult to entertain that possibility.

She dismissed Henry and The Comanche. Neither of them would have killed Maria. Thus, they had not killed Derek.

Who then?

Once again, her mind made its weary way through everything that had happened, tried to find a pattern that would offer an explanation to her.

The walls of the room oppressed her. The silence itself was threatening.

She had to speak to someone, to hear a voice, words.

She opened her door. The patio was still, empty. She saw a light in Richard's window.

Without waiting to think the impulse through, she hurried there. He opened the door at her knock. "Stacey? What is it?" There was quick alarm in his voice.

She slipped inside. "I wanted to ask you something."

The room seemed warm, comfortable, the littered desk a reassuring sight. "Were you working? Am I interrupting you?"

He shook his dark head. He leaned against the mantel, tall and lithe, broad-shouldered in his gray shirt. "Well?"

Her glance touched a chair.

"Sit down," he said more gently.

She was already regretting the impulse that had brought her there — the impulse that had followed swiftly on the heels of her unwilling suspicions of him. She was uneasily aware, suddenly, of his size, strength, and her vulnerability. She could think of nothing to say; and didn't want to admit to the loneliness that had brought her to this room.

He waited a moment. "Stacey, what is it?"

She raised her eyes to his, blurted, "Richard, was there ever anything between you . . . between you and Maria?"

Grim amusement shone in his eyes. "Don't you realize that might be an extremely dangerous question for you to ask me under certain circumstances?"

"It might be," she whispered. "But is it?"

"No. Now, listen, Stacey. You probably won't understand completely, but here it is. We all grew up together, Derek, Elena, John, Maria, and me. There was the age difference, of course. But for most of our lives we lived, always side by side, in this isolation. The others were close. I was the outsider. Don't ask me why. I don't know. Derek, Elena, and John were the real Alexanders and I remained the misfit. I got out as soon as I could. And, as for Maria . . ." he frowned. "I was sorry for Maria. I knew she'd never find happiness here. But she wouldn't leave, perhaps couldn't."

"I can understand that," Stacey said. "But then, if you'd left Casa de Sombra, why did you come back? Just then, Richard, two days after Derek and I arrived?"

"I wanted to see what was going on."

She stared at him, her disbelief rounding her wide blue eyes. "What made you think anything was going on?"

"I had my reasons."

There was a film of pink dust on the arm of the chair. She brushed it absently, then looked at her fingers.

"Adobe," he said.

She raised her eyes to his. "Would you do me a favor?"

"What?"

"The phone is in the living room, and any call that goes out is overheard." She drew a long breath. "Richard, call Bill Abel, ask him to come out here. I have to talk to him."

"For your sake, Stacey, I won't do it."

She felt as if she was sinking in a wave of hopelessness. With no one, no one to help her, she could not save herself. She forced herself to get to her feet.

He gave her a twisted smile. "Don't you remember, Stacey, I told you once not to trust anybody, not anybody."

"I'll remember," she promised him. "From now on, I'll remember."

At the door, she turned back to look at the chair. The smudge of pink adobe dust stood out on the green upholstery.

She was quite certain that the only pink

adobe in the Casa de Sombra was in those few bricks with the others at the foot of the patio near the gate.

The figure was small and in black, and when she turned her head, it disappeared.

She froze in brief mindless fear. A measureless instant passed before she realized that the menacing person she had glimpsed from the corner of her eye was herself. Trembling even after that recognition, she turned back to the mirror.

Her white face, dominated by wide frightened eyes, stared back at her. Her sandy curls were dishevelled.

The black skirt, the black blouse were mourning clothes.

Mourning for the Derek, who had, in truth, never existed. For the Derek that she had briefly thought she loved.

She turned away from the sight of her own anguish.

She must learn to forget Derek, forget what had happened.

The funeral had been mercifully short. John, Elena, and Richard had been ranged around her during the sad service, as if she might turn and flee. She had wanted to. But she knew it would be useless. Until Sheriff Abel told her she was free to go — if he ever did — she must stay in the Casa de Sombra.

Later, after the services, she had attended the two inquests with the family. They had also been mercifully short. It seemed as she and the others answered the questions put to them, that the coroner hardly listened. But before they left, he said, "Maria Santistevan was stabbed by persons unknown, hunh? And the same for Derek Alexander?" and looked at Bill Abel for approval. Bill gave a brief nod, a sideways glance at Stacey. Surrounded by the family, trembling, she got into the car, went back to the Casa de Sombra.

Now, with the day behind her, the late night silence full of menace, she paced her room, wondering how long it would be her cell, her sanctuary.

Suddenly, in mid-step, she paused. There had been a sound outside, a faint but distinct round. Listening, breath suspended, she heard it again.

She thought of the high whine of a car on the road near the gate, the silence when it stopped, the low moan of the iron hinge. Since the night of Maria's death, there had been no cars on the road. The gate had not been opened.

And now, Stacey thought, the midnight visitors might have come again. She rushed to the window, but from within, as always, there was nothing to see but the steep bank of shadows spread from wing to wing of the big house.

She tiptoed to the door, opened it.

Nothing but silence met her straining ears.

She hurried into the blackness, angling toward the gate.

She was nearly there, passing the stack of adobe bricks, when she heard a sound again. But this time it was behind her. A whisper only, but enough to stop her in her tracks. Before she could scream, turn, even take another breath, something soft, musty, thrusting, pulled against her face, pulled and held there so that she arched back and went down, breath sealed away from her, precious air withheld. Her flailing arms struck out, whipped emptiness, were caught, pinned. And then, within the bounds of the quick struggle, red haze drifted before her sealed eyes. Pain knifed at her throat. She sank away, dimly, dimly, into a new darkness . . .

She was aware, first of all, of pain. A great gouging pain at her throat. She saw the red haze, a haze in which she still drifted that thinned as she watched it. And then there were voices, faraway, whispering voices.

She strained and fought, and finally she was able to force her eyes open.

Richard was leaning over her, his lips white, face stony.

Beyond his bare wide shoulders, she saw the arc of blue sky, fading stars, the dark ridges of the mountains that surrounded the ravine.

"Better?" he asked softly.

She managed a faint, "Yes. I think so." Her voice was strange, rough-edged. The sound of it hurt her ears, making the sound hurt her throat. There was an odd burning at her back, her shoulders, her hips.

Elena cried, "Stacey, why this? What did you do?"

"Not now," Richard snapped.

He eased an arm around Stacey, a strong bare arm warm and secure, for her to lean against.

She saw the well rope cut and dangling. She saw the big knot that formed the swinging noose. There was a pillow, one that she recognized from the living room, among the crushed hollyhocks.

She knew then what had happened. The sound at the gate had been made deliberately to draw her there. Someone had watched her leave her room, had waited until she was past him, then followed her down to the patio. There, away from the house, the pillow had been pressed against her face, suffocating her, drawing the red haze before her eyes. And when she collapsed, she was dragged to the well, the noose dropped around her throat. The bucket . . .

She should have been found, like Derek, dangling limp, strangled, dead, above the shaft that seemed to lead into the heart of the earth.

She shuddered. Her wide blue eyes moved slowly around the circle. Elena, her face drawn, wore slim black pajamas of heavy cotton. John, fumbling with his mustache, wore a maroon robe. Richard was shirtless, in dark trousers. Beyond the family, Henry and The Comanche watched in stony silence, dressed by night as they were by day.

Stacey tried to remember what she had felt, struggling against the arms that seized her, what she had sensed before she fell into darkness. A firm, paralyzing grip. The mustiness of the suffocating pillow. That was all that was left to her of the terrible struggle.

"Easy," Richard said. He lifted her gently. "John, call the doctor in from Piedras."

Stacey whispered, "There's no need. I don't want a doctor." And as he carried her, holding her close, "Wait, Richard. I want to see."

"See what?" Elena asked. "What is it, Stacey?"

"At the gate. Where I was."

But Richard, not answering, carried her to

100

her room. For those few moments, she relished the security of his arms, taking an odd pleasure in the beat of his heart against her own.

But then, as he put her down on the bed, smoothed the blue coverlet over her, she remembered how Derek had looked, caught in the noose above the well.

Derek had died after she told him about the lie Richard had told Bill Abel. Derek had died after she had warned Richard that Derek knew the truth, and warned Richard, as well, that she was going to explain it all to Bill Abel. And now, she had herself been attacked. Did that prove that he had done it? Was he the masked enemy? Had he killed Maria, and his own brother?

He was leaning over her.

She shrank away from him.

He frowned, asked, "What did you want to see at the gate, Stacey?"

"It happened there. Someone came up behind me, put the pillow over my face. I think that when I'd passed out, I was dragged to the well, and . . ."

"Stacey," Elena said softly, "Stacey, you mustn't make up stories like that. Not for us. We all understand what happened."

"That's what happened. Just what I said," Stacey whispered. "Look there. You'll see the marks in the dust. Look at my clothes. You see? You see?"

No one answered.

"Maria first. Derek next. Now me," Stacey insisted. "Don't you understand?"

Elena gave her a pitying look. "Never mind, Stacey. We do understand, believe me. This has all been too much for you, and that fool Bill Abel . . ."

But, thought Stacey, it was Elena herself who had, somehow, without putting it into words, first accused Stacey.

John was nodding, his red mouth for once unsmiling. "This attack on you, as you call it, would have roused the house. You'd have fought, screamed. I heard nothing. Nor did Elena. Not until Richard shouted."

"You found me?" she asked him.

He nodded.

"How?"

"*I* did hear something. I don't know what. I came outside to look. I saw you there."

"And no one else?"

"No one, Stacey."

"You cut me down?"

"Yes."

She asked herself why, if he had tried to murder her, he had then saved her. Or was the attack merely to have been a warning?

"We'll have to tell Bill Abel about this, I'm

afraid," Elena murmured regretfully. "I'd rather not, Stacey. I'm sure you know that. But I'm afraid we will have to."

"The first thing in the morning," John said.

It was moments before she understood their barely concealed satisfaction. Then she realized that if she had been found dead, she would have been thought to have committed suicide.

She took a long slow breath. "I was not trying to kill myself," she said.

They didn't answer her.

But it was plain that they didn't believe her. They didn't want to. For suicide would imply guilt. And even attempted suicide implied guilt. The net of danger was firmly closed around her.

She leaned back, turned away from them.

Chapter Eleven

Bill Abel looked at the marks on her throat, at the torn, stained skirt and blouse she had been wearing the night before.

He listened patiently as she described what had happened to her.

She realized that she must control her terror, be precise, coherent. And to her own ears, she was unsuccessful. But she knew, by the narrowing of his blue eyes, by the way he whispered, "That takes a lot of believing," that the others had spoken to him first. Before he had come in with Richard to question her, he had been convinced that conscience had driven her to attempt suicide.

She made one last try. "Did you see the drag marks? They must have been there?"

"Maybe must of been, but weren't."

"Somebody could have brushed them away," she said in a small voice.

He leaned toward her. "'Who'd want to kill you, Stacey? What for?"

Any of the Alexanders, either of the two Indians. That was what was in her mind. But she had no proof to offer. And the motive she suspected . . . She drew a long slow breath. She must tell Bill Abel everything. Now, now . . .

And Richard said, "You've worn her out, Bill. That's enough. She doesn't know anything else to tell you."

She slid a sideways look at Richard. His cold gray eyes stared at her in obvious warning. He didn't want her to tell Bill about the lie. He didn't know about the rest of it. So it was the alibi he must be concerned with. Richard? Could it be Richard who walked, a silent shadow in the night?

Bill was saying, "You know as well as I do nobody set you up on that rope. Now don't you want to make it easy on yourself? Just tell us about it, and it'll be all over."

Again Richard cut in, "That's enough, Bill."

He sighed, rose. "Well then, why did you try to hang yourself?"

She saw that it was no use. She turned her face to the wall.

"I'll be back," he told her. "We'll get to talk some more."

She knew that he was not looking for the murderer of Maria and Derek, but only for some proof that would fix the guilt on her. The Alexanders were sacrosanct. He had known them all his life. She was the stranger.

"Wait," she said.

He paused at the door.

Richard asked, "What is it, Stacey?"

She ignored Richard, demanded of Bill, "Do I have to stay here? Can't I move into town?"

He looked embarrassed, his blue eyes narrowed. "I guess you can move to town if you want to. But why would you?"

She didn't bother to answer him.

He said uneasily, "Listen, what I meant was, you only got to stay in the county. If you're not mixed up in this, like you say, you got nothing to worry about."

"I haven't?" she asked bitterly.

"Now wait a minute. I'm not railroading you. If I were, you'd be in jail by now. Don't you know that?"

Richard pulled the door open. "Come on, Bill," and let Bill go ahead. Turning back, he told Stacey, "You'll feel better after a while, I'm sure."

By evening, the bruises at her throat were shades of yellow and blue. She covered them with a high-necked blouse the same color as her eyes. She put on a narrow skirt of the same shade. She made up carefully. It was all a matter of finding enough courage, she told herself.

Her only safety lay in escaping from the Casa de Sombra. Away from the watchful gray eyes of Richard, she could tell Bill Abel everything that she knew. She could, perhaps, convince him of the truth.

It wouldn't be easy to get the Alexanders to drive her into Piedras, she knew. But since there was no other way, she had to try.

That night at dinner, steeling herself to it, she approached Elena.

There was a brief silence.

The candlelight flickered.

Elena toyed with a fork.

John sipped his wine.

Richard's gray eyes were narrow and watchful.

Then Elena said, "Bill told you you mustn't leave, Stacey. And I know you want to get it straightened out."

"I can stay in town until then."

"But why would you do that? This is your home, Stacey." John had taken it up. "You *are* Derek's widow. Whatever happened can't change that. And you deserve Derek's share. As head of the family, I shall see that you get it."

She recognized his words as a discreet bribe. She said, "I don't want anything, John."

"My dear, that's unwise of you. You can't realize what you're rejecting."

"It doesn't matter. I prefer to leave."

"What makes you think you'll be better off there than here?" Richard demanded.

"I will be safer," she told him bluntly.

"Oh, my poor Stacey," Elena murmured, with a sidelong look at John.

It was useless, Stacey knew. They would not allow her to leave the Casa de Sombra. From the beginning, they had feared her presence there, but had feared even more that she would go.

She remembered the conversation she had heard between Elena and Derek when she heard Elena say, "You must be nicer, else she'll go away." Derek had retorted, "Never mind. I can manage her." And Elena said, "But we can't take chances."

She remembered the bits of other conversations she had heard, John's suspicious look when he saw her watching, listening to Maria and Derek.

They were all of them afraid that she knew, had guessed something about Derek, about what had made him marry her, about the Casa de Sombra itself.

"You would be safer with us, surely, from whatever it is that you fear than alone," John was saying.

She decided not to argue. The Alexanders wouldn't give in. She supposed that she had not really expected them to.

She must find a way to leave. But on her own, with help from no one.

She was relieved when dinner was over, relieved to escape from those three pairs of watchful eyes.

She excused herself, started for her room.

Richard followed her. "Don't try it, Stacey."

She didn't answer.

"I can watch out for you here. Not in Piedras."

"You can watch out for me?" She stopped, looked up into his stony face. "Don't you really mean that next time you'll do a better job?"

She didn't wait for a reply. She walked away through the purple twilight, keeping her eyes turned resolutely away from the well.

But at the door of her room, she stopped, listened.

Yes. Yes. She heard it clearly.

It wasn't a fanciful wish. It wasn't imagination.

She ran, following the sound to its source, The Comanche's quarters.

Chapter Twelve

She knocked, thrust open the door.

The weeping was louder.

She tiptoed in.

A big carved cradle stood in a corner beside a narrow cot.

Stacey leaned over the cradle. Huge black eyes peered up at her. A small rosebud mouth slowly closed, then spread in a wide grin. The tiny copper-colored face so clearly showed the mixture of two races that Stacey needed no one to tell her that this child, smiling so joyfully at her now, had been Maria's child. Maria's and Derek's. Or — and the thought struck her with sudden pain — Maria's and Richard's.

So here was the source of that infant wail which Derek had said must be her wild imagination. This was why she had been warned away from the wing across the patio. And this was why Maria had hated her. Maria had hated her . . . because of Derek. The child was Derek's.

Stacey spun around at the slight sound behind her.

Henry and The Comanche stood in the doorway.

"Yes," The Comanche said, her mouth spread in a toothless grin. "Yes. Now you know the truth. He is Maria's son by Derek Alexander."

Stacey couldn't move. She breathed slowly, fearfully. The two faces, usually so expressionless, were graven now with hate.

"You came . . . you with your blue eyes . . ." Henry spat on the floor. "You. Yes. He had promised to marry Maria when he returned from that last trip to Mexico. His last trip, he said, and then he would marry Maria. Instead, he brought you. And in the house where she was to have been mistress, Maria was made a servant again. A servant to be hidden away with her child."

"And now Maria is dead," The Comanche said softly.

"But Derek . . . he, too, is dead," Henry answered.

Stacey moved toward the door. "I didn't know," she whispered. "Surely you realize that I never knew this about Maria."

The two Indians stepped aside. They didn't speak.

Stacey was too shocked to be frightened then.

It was only when she was back in her room that she asked herself if she had stumbled upon a motive that could explain everything. Had they killed Maria, their only daughter, because she had dishonored them? Had they then killed Derek? And was Stacey herself, as the third part of the triangle, to be their next victim?

The shadow on the Casa de Sombra seemed darker than ever. The violet twilight had faded. Faint streaks of sunset disappeared beyond the mountain ridges as she watched from the window.

She knew that she must find some way to escape.

John was walking toward her, ambling along beneath the portales, smoking a cigar.

She moved quickly away from the window.

It was hours later. At last the faint blur of lights showing from behind the draped windows had gone out.

The patio was dark, still.

Yet Stacey hesitated, wanting to be certain that no one was watching in the shadows.

The rope burns stung at her throat, a sharp reminder of the night before. She remembered too clearly the attack that had come out of the dark.

She was afraid to leave the dubious safety of her room, yet it was impossible to remain there.

She didn't know how — from whom, from

where — another attack would come. But that it would come, and soon, she did know.

She had increased her own danger by asking the Alexanders to take her in to Piedras, by not telling Bill Abel all that she knew when she had the chance.

Her only safety lay in escape from the Casa de Sombra.

She pictured the road that lay ahead, long, curving, dark, unfamiliar. But she reminded herself that once she had covered those miles to the end of the ravine, she would be on the highway. There she could hope that someone would drive by, give her a lift into the town.

She made herself put on her topcoat. She took her bag. Listening for a long moment at the door, she heard nothing but the quick rhythm of her heart. Then, with a small silent prayer, she went out, tiptoed from under the portales to the dusty patio. She knew the way now. She could avoid the well, the cluster of hollyhocks, the neat pile of adobe brick near the wall. Breathless, shivering, she made it to the gate.

The huge iron hinge gave a familiar squeal as she swung the heavy cedar gate open. Slowly, carefully, she closed it behind her.

She was away, running down the narrow road, slipping, sliding, yet managing to keep to her feet.

The sky was a deep, star-sprinkled blue, spreading black to the mountain ridges. A tiny crescent moon glowed faintly silver far away.

She wanted to laugh for joy, to sing.

The Casa de Sombra was behind her.

It was nothing more now than a bulking shadow set in the ravine.

Though it was miles to Piedras, and she didn't know how she would get there, she was exhilarated by a sense of freedom.

Was it a month since she had come to the Casa de Sombra with Derek? Just a month? It seemed as if she had lived with terror all her life.

Gasping, she ran on past the first great swinging curve, into it, around it.

She remembered riding into town with Richard, laughing in the sudden sunlight, talking over chocolate sodas. It had been a good day, the only good day she remembered since her arrival, since she and Derek had crossed from sun into the shadow of the ravine. Richard . . . There had been a peculiar pleasure in his touch, an odd joy, easing her pain, when he had carried her close to his heart the night before. But there had been menace in his low hard voice, his gray eyes. And the lie he had told for her had been for himself, too.

A stitch in her side slowed her down. A heaviness in her breath dragged her feet. She stopped for a moment, sucking in long draughts of the cool, sweet air. Then she forced herself to go on, taking brisk, brave steps in the darkness.

She had reached the edge of the ravine. Just beyond her, she saw the faint outline of jagged rock that opened onto the highway. But it was wrong. Something big, dark, formed an obstruction.

She stopped, straining to see. A faint wink of light, gone almost as quickly as it appeared, warned her.

She gasped, swung away from the road. In that moment, great white beams caught her. She was impaled on twin knives of light.

Fright blossomed in her, a quick, searing flame.

Someone was waiting for her.

Someone had read her thoughts, and gone ahead of her.

But who? Who?

She spun away, flung herself from the knives of light, seeking the safety of the dark which always before she had feared. Off the road, mesquite tore at her legs, long grass brushed her face with ghostly fingers.

Over the loud rasp of her agonized breath, she heard the sound of pursuit.

She heard pounding footsteps, a quick whisper.

Hands seized her from behind.

She threw herself sideways and fell.

The hands seized her again, hard, biting hands that caught and held her.

Sobbing, limp, she suddenly realized that the quick whisper had become words, words she could understand.

"Stacey, Stacey, don't. Don't be afraid of me."

It was Richard, leaning over her, holding her.

"You!" she cried.

"Quietly. Please."

She pulled away from his encircling arms. "It was you all the time," she whispered. "I didn't want to believe it. But I knew . . . I guessed . . ."

"Stacey . . ."

"What are you waiting for then?"

A quick grin flashed across his face. "To talk to you. If you'll be quiet and listen."

"To talk to me," she said contemptuously. "You could have done that in the house."

"I knew you would try it. So did the rest of them. We don't have much time, Stacey. Will you listen to me?"

"There's nothing to listen to, Richard. I'm going in to Piedras. I'm going to tell Bill Abel everything. Everything, do you understand me?"

"Everything?" Richard took her arm. "Come on."

"But where?"

"To the car."

She hung back. "What for, Richard?"

He gave her a light push. "If I intended to kill you, and obviously that's what you expect, don't you realize that I would have done it, and easily, by now?"

She went with him silently to the car.

He helped her in, but first he plucked a long blade of grass from her hair, gently smoothed her sandy curls. "I didn't mean to frighten you. I thought I'd see you in time, and let you know it was me, and . . ."

"You were smoking a cigarette," she said. "I saw a tiny flicker of light."

"And took off like a rabbit." He settled down beside her. "Not that I blame you after everything that's happened."

"And now?" she asked hopelessly.

"I want you to come back to Casa de Sombra with me."

"I won't, Richard." She added softly, "Not willingly. I have to see Bill Abel. Now. Tonight."

"To tell him . . . tell him what, Stacey?"

"All of it." She drew a long, slow breath. "There's a lot I don't know, don't understand. But . . . listen, Richard, Derek didn't marry me for love. He needed a wife, a woman to be with him on that trip around Mexico. I was . . . I was vulnerable, so he chose me.

I was a . . . a cover for him. I don't know exactly why, or what he was doing. But I think he was smuggling something . . . I think . . . Anyway, when we got here, he didn't need me any more. So he dropped the masquerade."

"You *did* know it then," Richard said. "I kept hoping . . ."

"And I'm going to tell Bill Abel."

"No, Stacey, no!" His big hands bruised her shoulders. "That's just what you can't do. I've known him all my life. Believe me. You say that much and he'll run out to Casa de Sombra and say, 'Listen, you want to hear the wildest thing . . .' and give it all away to Elena and John. Then we'd never know the truth!"

"But do you want to?" she asked steadily. "Why should you want to? You're mixed up in it yourself!"

"Not the way you think, Stacey." He paused. "Oh, I know how it looks to you. But you're wrong."

His fingers were still biting in her shoulders. She tried to pull away. "You're hurting me, Richard."

He let go of her. "Sorry, Stacey."

"Will you drive me into Piedras?"

He shook his head.

"Then you are mixed up in it!"

He turned to look at her. A dark lock fell

118

over his forehead. He said gently, "Stacey, you won't ever be safe, don't you understand? Not until we discover who killed Maria and Derek. You know too much about the Alexanders. And they already know that. Don't you remember what happened last night?"

"I remember it," she whispered.

"And Derek, whatever he was, was also my brother, Stacey."

"Not for my safety then."

Richard stared at her. "Don't you know?"

"Know what?" she demanded.

He smiled slightly, a smile quickly gone. "Never mind that for now. I had hoped that you didn't understand but since you do, well, I'd better explain." He stopped, lit a cigarette, then went on, "In my business, working for the paper, I hear things. Do you know what I mean? Small whispers, rumors, word that goes around. You never know what to believe. The sources aren't always trustworthy, and the word here and there doesn't always make sense. But anyway, I heard it said that for a price, with the right contact, a man could buy heroin at Casa de Sombra. Enough heroin imported from Mexico to make himself a fortune. Naturally, I didn't believe it at first. I guess I just didn't want to. But the rumors kept coming. Finally I heard that Derek had come back, and come back married."

"Heroin," Stacey whispered.

He nodded.

"The cars outside, the gate hinge in the night."

He nodded again. "Easily transportable, easily sold. The rumors had mentioned the house, the product, not the source. But I had to discount Henry and The Comanche. Neither of them go to Mexico. So . . . so it was one of the family then. Or . . . maybe it was all of them."

"You came home when you heard that Derek had come back."

"As soon as I could get here. I wanted to know what was going on, to put a stop to it. Before I saw you, I thought that you were his knowing accomplice. But when I did see you, I realized that you'd been duped. Yes, duped, Stacey. You're right about that. My brother used you, I'm sure of that, to keep everyone from being suspicious of him. Who expects a man on his honeymoon to be smuggling heroin into the country? He may have thought he was being watched by the Treasury Department, or by Customs. But anyway, that's what he did and brought you back here. Derek, having chosen you himself, was absolutely sure of you. And besides, being sure of himself, he assumed he could do anything he wanted with you. But Elena or John, or maybe both of them together, were suspicious of what you knew or guessed. They didn't want you in Casa de Sombra, yet they couldn't let you leave. Not until the distribution of the heroin was completed, so that they could all go on a nice long trip."

"Leave me dead," Stacey whispered.

"Perhaps."

"But then Maria was killed . . . The sounds in the night stopped, Richard."

He nodded.

"Maria had a baby. Did you know?"

"Yes, I suppose you thought it was mine."

"At first. But I realized that Maria hated me. And that wouldn't have made sense unless the baby was Derek's. And then Henry and The Comanche told me the truth."

"Maria . . ." he said bitterly. "Poor little girl. She loved him too much. She was angry with him. And she knew, you see. She must have known about the gate opening in the night, the darkened car."

"But who killed her? Which of them, Richard?"

"I don't know. Not any more than I know who killed Derek. And that's why I need your help, Stacey."

She understood. She said slowly, "As bait, Richard?"

"Yes, I'm afraid so. And I know what I'm

asking. But I've watched. And I'll continue to."

She believed him, yet there was still a faint doubt in her. "Why didn't you tell me all this before? Why didn't you warn me when you first came here, Richard?"

"Don't think I didn't want to, Stacey. I . . . well, I had to be sure. I've spent the month looking for the stuff. I know it has to be somewhere around. I thought if I got my hands on it, destroyed it, I could stop them. And all along, I've been sure that the less you knew the safer you'd be."

"But why, last night, did . . . someone . . . ?"

"They're in a hurry, Stacey. They want to get out now. I've been checking your room, the patio, often. And when I saw you there . . ." He stopped. He went on, his voice ragged, "I found the drag marks, Stacey."

"Then you really did alibi me to protect me from Bill, didn't you, Richard?"

"Of course," he said. "Though I took the risk of letting you think I needed that alibi myself."

"But I told Derek." She paused, thinking. "He must have passed that on to the others." She paused again "It's so ugly, Richard. All of it is so ugly."

"That's why I must end it. That's why I

have to know the truth."

"All right, Richard. Let's go back. Let's do what we have to do," she said.

She said the words in a soft steady voice, but she was breathless with fright. She had listened to him, listened and been convinced that he was to be trusted.

And now, suddenly, when he leaned towards her, brushed his lips on hers, she was no longer afraid.

She wanted to throw her arms around him, to cling to his strength. Yet an instant reaction, some instinct within her made her freeze. She thought of Derek winning her with kisses. She thought of the vulnerability, the hope for love, which had brought her to the Casa de Sombra. She asked herself if the same thing was happening to her again.

"All right, Stacey." Richard's voice was deep, angry. "I know how you feel. But trust me this much, in spite of my family, trust me to protect you."

Chapter Thirteen

He was with her in the long day that followed.

At breakfast, Elena said, "Why, Stacey, you do look so worn this morning. You must rest."

And John, smoothing his mustache, chuckled, "Don't worry, Stacey. Everything is going to be all right."

The Comanche and Henry moved silently on moccasined feet, serving coffee, their swarthy faces as blank as always.

Richard smiled at her across the table.

For a few moments, she forgot that she was bait in a death trap. For a few moments, she was able to smile in return. But the respite was too short, Richard's almost constant presence through the long slow hours too much of a reminder.

At last, the shadow over the Casa de Sombra thickened with night darkness.

She went to her room.

She lay on the big, blue-canopied bed, dressed, waiting, certain that her terror would be an antidote to exhaustion, certain that she would never sleep again. But as the hours drifted slowly by, as the night stillness lay more and more heavily on the house, her wide eyes closed. Her stiff body slowly relaxed. She listened to the whisper of wind in the holly-hocks, and it turned to sweet music as she drifted into sleep . . .

She felt the movement, heard it, within a hazy dream. A movement too close, too threatening. She wakened and threw her head back, and the pain of cold metal sliced along her cheek. She cried out.

"Be quiet," Elena whispered. "Be very quiet, Stacey."

Elena, with dark eyes shining, stood beside the big bed. She held a gun, its hungry barrel pressed to Stacey's throat.

She had known that it must happen. That either John or Elena would come for her. Yet she couldn't really believe that the trap had sprung. She turned desperate eyes toward the door.

"He won't be here," Elena said. "If you're looking for Richard, forget it."

The terror was swift, painful. It sucked Stacey's breath from her, left her a husk, a dead thing. "You've killed him," she whispered.

"Why, no, Stacey. Whatever for? It's just that there will be a small diversion. Provided for by John." Her voice hardened, lost its soft musical note. "Get up, Stacey. I mean it. Now."

Stacey rose slowly.

Elena stepped back a pace, the gun steady in her hand.

"You're dressed, aren't you?" She laughed softly. "Perhaps you were even expecting me."

"Yes," Stacey agreed. "I was expecting you."

Richard had been going to protect her. Where was he? What would John do to him? She asked Elena in a fierce whisper, "Is Richard all right?"

"Of course." Elena laughed again. "Why not?"

The words were out before Stacey could stop them, before she realized that they put him in jeopardy. She said, "But he knows the truth, Elena."

"Of course," Elena said again. "That's why he came home in the first place. But he can't prove a thing. Nothing at all. So, suspecting, knowing it doesn't matter, the only thing he can do is go away. And that's what he'll do. Once it's over."

Stacey stood very still, stiff with fright, listening, straining to hear the sound of Richard's low, hard voice, straining for a clue to what was happening to him.

"Let's go," Elena said. "Everything is waiting on us, you know."

Stacey reached for the coat she had left at the foot of the bed.

"You won't need it. It will be over in no time. First we're going to Derek's room. That's a good touch, isn't it? Where you will be found in the morning, a poor suicide, guilt-ridden to her death!"

Time, Stacey thought. *She must give Richard time.*

And she moved toward the door, and Elena followed, the gun steady in her hand.

Stacey asked in a dry whisper, "Elena, why this? Why?"

"So many reasons. Where do I begin? You know too much, of course. And you killed him. You killed him, Stacey!"

"No, Elena. I didn't. Don't you see? Don't you realize I couldn't have killed Derek?"

"It must have been you. You were jealous of Maria. You understood what had gone on, even if you hadn't seen the baby yet. And Derek wouldn't pretend to be your true husband any more. He wouldn't cooperate. Poor Derek, he just wouldn't listen to me. Not about you, not even about Maria. Though I warned him what she would do."

"What Maria would do, Elena?"

"She was going to go away. She would have told everything."

"Everything about the smuggling?"

"Yes. And that's why I killed her."

"You!"

"You went to Derek's room. I watched. I got Maria to go with me to yours, and I stabbed her there. I wanted you to be blamed for that. And you played into my hands, admitting you intended to leave Derek. Richard lied for you, of course. But that didn't matter. Bill Abel suspected you. But he didn't arrest you right away, which was lucky for us. I realized you had to stay here, until we were finished. And then . . ."

"You, Elena," Stacey said in wonderment, "you with the pillow."

"Of course. But I couldn't quite finish it, which was such a shame. Richard found you in time."

The gun pressed harder into Stacey's throat.

She moved obediently. She stepped through the door, allowed Elena to nudge her down the walk.

She glanced toward the gate. It was swinging open. A light flickered there. The high whine of a car drifted on the night.

"Not a sound," Elena whispered. "Not a sound."

She pushed Stacey ahead of her, pushed her quickly through the shadows to Derek's room.

Stacey went ahead, one step, then two, dragging her feet in the dust, waiting for the blow, the pain, the end.

The car's whine faded as Elena closed the

door, sealing the two of them within the empty dark.

"Our little diversion worked," she said.

The gun thrust against Stacey's throat, directed her toward the bed.

"Maria . . . if it hadn't been for her." Elena's taut whisper was suddenly full of hate. "Her and her baby. We would have been all right. In spite of you, Stacey. He had promised to marry her, but he brought you here. You were safe, he insisted. You knew nothing. He suspected he was being followed. You were the answer. But we'd had word that there were others who wanted what he was collecting. When he brought you, we thought you might be with those others. And then it didn't matter. For you heard the baby cry, Maria's baby. You were suspicious of all of us. And Maria . . . she would have told Bill Abel."

Stacey thought she saw a flash of movement, a flicker of light at the window. She turned away from it. She moved on the bed. "But I didn't kill Derek," she whispered. "So who did?"

"You must have." Elena sounded bewildered. Then, with her voice hardening, she went on, "But he's gone. And now John and I must look after ourselves."

"The heroin," Stacey said hopelessly.

"Of course."

"It was all for money then, wasn't it?"

"Of course it was for money. What else? We needed it. There was nothing, nothing left. We were the biggest family in the state for generations. And then there was nothing. That was all right for Richard. He didn't care. But the rest of us . . ."

"You pretended so well."

"I'll pretend well tomorrow, too," Elena said.

Stacey gave a swift glance toward the window, then closed her eyes lest Elena noticed within them a sudden flare of hope.

Outside, against the night, strange shadows leaped and danced. Strange shadows moved like living flame. Fire. Somewhere in the night there was fire.

Stacey lay back on the bed, her hands raised, fingers clenched into the pillows. Richard, she thought. Richard, please . . .

"Now," Elena murmured, leaning forward.

And Stacey slapped the pillow up, flung it as hard as she could into Elena's face. At the same time, as she threw herself aside, she saw the door burst open.

From the midst of the smoky pink light that drifted in, Richard appeared and seized Elena.

Screaming, struggling, she tore away from him, backed to the door, the gun pointed at him.

"You should have stayed there snooping at the open gate, waiting, the way John thought you would," she cried.

"This won't do you any good, Elena." He put his hands out to her. "Give it up. Give it all up. Now."

"And then?"

But Richard didn't have time to answer her.

John lurched into the open doorway. "Elena! The house is burning. It's over, Elena!"

"No!" she screamed.

The gun moved in a quick terrifying arc. Richard threw himself at her.

But the gun went off as she collapsed under his weight.

Stacey heard the sharp sound, felt the sudden driving pain in her shoulder. She staggered back, clung to the wall.

John bent, fumbled along the floor.

She tried to shout a warning.

But it was too late. When John rose, he had the gun.

"We're going," he said softly. "You're not going to stop us either."

Elena rose, smoothing the dark shining coils of her hair. She stepped away from Richard, nodded at John. "Mexico. Yes. We can start again."

They moved together, moved through the

pink smoke, in the patio, under the flaming portales.

Richard caught Stacey in his arms, carried her outside.

"Let them go," she whispered. "Please, Richard . . ."

"Yes." He held her against him gently. And then, holding her, he began to run, angling for the gate.

John and Elena had stopped at the end of the portales. They were outlined in pink light, blowing embers drifted down from the flaming roof. And beyond them, standing before the pile of tan and pink adobe brick, was a short, broad figure.

"No." The word was loud, sharp. "You cannot have it."

"Henry, get out of the way," John yelled.

"You two, you did it," Henry said. "You, Elena, you killed my Maria. It was you. Not Derek, as I thought. The Comanche heard him. She heard him say, 'If you make trouble, I promise I'll kill you! I'll kill you! I promise!' The Comanche heard him. And Maria was killed. So he had to die. He died with the rope at his throat as he deserved, and looking into my eyes with terror. But it was you, Elena, not him, that did it. You feared she would tell the truth about the adobe bricks."

"It won't do you any good to know that.

Get away, Henry," John growled.

"The fire," Henry told him. "I made the fire. You were here at the gate, drawing Richard here. So I made the fire. Now you understand. The Casa de Sombra will be gone for good." The swarthy face wrinkled in a smile. "I knew you would come here. For the evil you have hidden in your tan brick."

The night wind blew a lick of flame along the old vegas of the portales. It crackled a sudden warning.

Elena screamed.

John raised the gun. The brief sound was hard, ugly. But it was lost almost immediately in the crash of the crumbling portales.

As Henry fell, a red stain blossoming on his shirt, the roof came down.

Stacey, clinging to Richard, and watching in horror, couldn't believe her eyes. One moment, Elena and John were silhouetted by pink light. The next they were gone, buried, and all around them flames leaped high.

Epilogue

Bill Abel had been and gone, taking The Comanche and Maria's son with him, taking the adobe bricks in which the heroin had been hidden. "I'd never have believed it," he insisted.

There were streaks of sunrise on the mountain ridges around the ravine. The smoking ruins were shrouded in shadow. There was nothing left of the Casa de Sombra when Richard and Stacey drove away from it.

At the highway, they stopped to look back. "That was all they wanted," Richard said. "To keep the house, the old life going. Now it's finished. Forget them, Stacey. Forget you ever knew them." He bent his dark head, kissed her lightly.

Then they drove into the sunlight together.